The Shapeshifter's Guide to Running Away

Also by LARI DON

Spellchasers Trilogy
The Beginner's Guide to Curses
The Shapeshifter's Guide to Running Away
The Witch's Guide to Magical Combat

Fabled Beast Chronicles
First Aid for Fairies and Other Fabled Beasts
Wolf Notes and Other Musical Mishaps
Storm Singing and Other Tangled Tasks
Maze Running and Other Magical Missions

Rocking Horse War

For older readers
Mind Blind

For younger readers
The Big Bottom Hunt
How to Make a Heron Happy
The Magic Word
Orange Juice Peas

The Secret of the Kelpie
The Tale of Tam Linn

Spellchasers

The Shapeshifter's Guide to Running Away

LARI DON

Kelpies is an imprint of Floris Books
First published in 2017 by Floris Books
First published in the USA in 2017
© 2017 Lari Don

The publisher acknowledges subsidy from
Creative Scotland towards the publication
of this volume

 Also available
as an eBook

British Library CIP Data available
ISBN 978-178250-306-4
Printed in England by Clays Ltd, St Ives plc

For Mirren

Thank you for never getting too big for this kind of magic. I will always write these stories for you, even when you're off having your own adventures

Chapter One

Molly's curse got worse early on Sunday morning.

Molly expected to become human as she leapt through the air.

She expected to beat Innes to the finish line as a hare, change shape when she crossed the stone wall into Aunt Doreen's garden, and crash-land on the ground as a girl.

That's what always happened.

She always beat her friend Innes when he challenged her to a race. She always controlled her curse by crossing a boundary and becoming human again, just in time to accept his grudging congratulations.

But this time, when she landed on the ground, she didn't fall and bash her knees. This time she stayed on all four feet. All four paws.

She was over the wall, over the boundary, and she was still a hare. Still small, vulnerable, defenceless. Still unable to speak.

Innes thumped down on his heavy hooves, shapeshifted from white horse to blond boy, then said, "Well done.

Again. Though I don't know how you do it. I was the fastest thing in Speyside until you arrived. You weigh less than one of my hooves, you don't even train, and you still beat me every single time. It's not… fair. But, obviously, well done, again."

Molly couldn't answer.

Innes sighed. "Why have you shifted back to a hare already? Do you want another race? I will beat you eventually, but I'm not giving it another go until I've had one of your great-aunt's biscuits. So bounce over the wall and become a girl again. You're easier to chat to when you can talk back."

Molly turned and jumped over the wall, hoping it had been some kind of magical blip, hoping the rules of her curse would work as usual this time.

She landed in the field neatly and elegantly. She was still a hare.

Over the past week, Molly had got used to being a part-time hare. She enjoyed the speed and the strength of her long hare legs and she loved beating Innes in races. But she didn't want to be a full-time hare.

She'd learnt to manipulate this curse, with the help of her new friends. She'd discovered that, as well as becoming a hare unwillingly when she heard a dog bark or growl, she could choose to shift from human to hare by growling like a dog herself. She also knew that she always shifted back from hare to human when she crossed the boundary between one owner's land and the next: a garden wall, a playground fence, a road cutting between two farms. So why wasn't it working now?

She leapt the wall again, still enjoying the power of her legs and the precision of her senses, but also starting to feel trapped inside this small fragile shape. She landed, on all four paws. She was still a hare.

Molly looked down at her delicate brown paws, wondering if she'd ever see her pale human fingers again.

Innes was frowning. "Why are you still a hare?" He crouched down and placed a hand gently on her back.

With his warm palm on her spine, Molly was suddenly aware of her fast jerky breathing. Stuck inside this hare body, she was beginning to panic.

"Calm down, Molly. We'll work this out. Maybe this wall is, I don't know, broken or something. Let's try other boundaries..."

Innes wrapped his hands round her ribcage, about to pick her up. Molly flicked her ears in annoyance, slid out of his grasp and sprinted across her aunt's garden. She leapt over the hens' wire run, hurdled the wooden fence into Mr Buchan's weeds, then jumped a white wall onto the Websters' lawn.

She was still a hare.

She swerved round in a tight circle and ran back. Over the wall, over the fence, round the confused chickens, back to Innes.

"So walls don't work and fences don't work," he said, "even though they worked yesterday. We'll have to change you back another way." He paused. "I shift by thinking about the shape I want to be. Why don't you try that?"

Molly's ears drooped. Innes changed easily because he was a kelpie, a born shapeshifter, able to become human or horse or fish or monster at will. She'd been cursed to change from human to hare, so she had much less control over her shapeshifting.

"I know," said Innes, "it's probably not as easy for you. But see if it works."

Molly closed her wide-vision eyes and pictured herself. Her girl-self. The self she had been every minute of every day until Mr Crottel had cursed her. She saw freckles and fingers. She saw bruised knees, poky elbows and short brown hair. She focused and she wished and she hoped.

And it made no difference at all. She was still a hare.

"This is beyond us," said Innes. "Let's ask Mrs Sharpe. She knows a lot more than she taught us on that curse-lifting workshop. If your curse has got worse somehow, she'll know what to do. Let's go to Skene Mains farm."

They walked down the narrow garden, through the back door into the kitchen, then crept through the bright cottage. As Innes opened the front door, Molly heard her Aunt Doreen call from the living room. "I'm off to Elgin soon to get some messages, so I'll not be back until teatime. See you later, Molly."

Innes muttered, "Alright. Bye," and dashed through the front door before Molly's aunt could identify his voice.

He shut the door and put Molly down on the pavement

in front of the row of houses between the distillery and the town.

He asked, "Would you rather go to Skene Mains the long way round town on your own paws, or the short way through town under my coat?"

She pointed her nose at the hills.

He grinned. "Race you?"

She shook her ears.

He sighed. "Ok. I know. On unfamiliar territory you have to be sensible, you have to keep an eye out for predators and snares. No race then; let's just meet at the farm gates. I bet I'll get there before you!"

Molly sprinted over the empty road, then into the fields that would take her in a long curve round the town of Craigvenie to Mrs Sharpe's farm.

As Molly ran at a comfortable speed, looking out for dogs, foxes and barbed wire, she realised Innes was galloping one field higher up, looking for more challenging obstacles to leap.

Each time she pushed under a gate or leapt a wall, she hoped to hit the ground with a human-sized crash. But each time, she was still a hare.

Then she ran into a grassy field and saw a moving shape to her left.

Was it a predator? A fox?

Molly dropped to the ground and lay flat, hiding her soft brown contours in the folds of the field. Then she recognised the shape.

It was a hare. Three hares. Long-legged and long-eared, like larger stronger faster rabbits. Silhouetted clearly on the grass of the field.

Molly had never met any other hares. She wondered if these hares would think she was a real hare, or only a pretend one.

She watched them.

They were grazing together, moving around each other, not too close, but clearly comfortable as a group.

They were all female. Molly wasn't sure how she knew that. But she did know it, even more clearly than she'd know whether a distant teenager in jeans and t-shirt was a boy or a girl.

These were girl hares.

So she moved towards them.

She knew they could see her. Her own vision was so wide she could see almost everything around her, except just in front of her nose and just behind her head. The hares had stopped cropping the grass. They were all standing very still.

Then the largest hare turned round to watch Molly approaching.

Was there a hare language? Molly wondered. Would she understand it?

Molly loped closer.

The other two hares turned round.

She moved even closer. Slowly. Not wanting to scare them.

But they didn't seem scared. They didn't seem suspicious or puzzled. They just stared at her.

The largest hare loped towards her. Molly tried to look friendly, with no idea what a hare would think was friendly. The hare reached Molly and stood up, showing her pale belly. Molly nodded a greeting.

The large hare punched her. Just whacked her, right on the nose. And again. And again. Punching, boxing, hitting.

Molly squealed, a noise she hadn't known she could make, and backed off.

She raised her own front paws, planning to fight back. Then she realised this hare was just defending her territory, or her babies, or her grass, or something else important to a real wild hare. Molly didn't want any of those things. Molly didn't want to fight her.

So when the hare bobbed forward to punch her again, Molly turned and ran away. She ran as fast as she could, away from the hares, towards the witch's farm, hoping with all her heart, for the first time, that she could lift this curse, and that she wouldn't have to spend her life trying to make friends with hares who punched her before even getting to know her.

She ran, knowing the only native animal in Scotland that could overtake her – a larger hare – was right behind her. But as she darted under the gate, the other hares were already nibbling grass again. Like she hadn't even been there.

Molly sprinted across the last few fields to Mrs Sharpe's farm. And she thought about grass. She'd never eaten as a hare. She'd always changed back in time to eat human food. If she was stuck as a hare, would she have to eat grass?

She stopped and looked at the grass under her paws. She bent down and sniffed the sour salad smell.

No. She wasn't hungry enough. She'd try eating grass later if she absolutely had to.

As she ran through the last field, Innes joined her, sweating from his gallop and jumps.

Molly knew that even though she was faster than Innes, she wasn't a true shapeshifter like him. He was equally at home as a horse or a boy. She wasn't really a hare. Perhaps it was time to accept that: to say goodbye to the speed and freedom of being a hare. Perhaps she really did have to find a way to lift this curse forever.

She leapt over the fence into the road, and ran between Mrs Sharpe's gateposts.

She felt an unfamiliar fizzing in her bones, tumbled forward in an uncontrolled somersault and caught a wide-angle glimpse of fur-covered paws stretching into long bony fingers. Then her vision narrowed, her hands hit the ground and her palms scraped painfully across the gravel.

Molly was a girl again.

But it had never happened like that before. She'd never seen herself shift from one shape to another; it usually happened too fast.

Molly shivered. Her curse had definitely got worse.

Chapter Two

"That makes no sense." Innes watched as Molly clambered to her feet and picked grit out of her palms. "Why did you change here? What's different about Mrs Sharpe's gate? You went through lots of gates on the way."

"Let's ask her." Molly walked up the track towards the farm shop, relieved she was a girl again and hoping her curse might soon return to its usual manageable magic. She also hoped Innes hadn't seen what happened in the grassy field.

But he grinned and started jabbing her in the arm with his fist. "So, you win races, but you don't win boxing matches. What did you do to annoy them? Did you say something rude?"

She pushed his hand away. "I didn't say anything. I just wanted to see if I could communicate with them."

"They certainly communicated with you. The 'Get out of our field NOW!' was pretty clear. Are you ok?"

"Fine. It was better than meeting a fox. Or a curse-hatched crow, or a grumpy wyrm, or any of the other things that have attacked me recently. It was certainly better than when you tried to drown me in your river."

Innes muttered, "I wasn't trying to drown you, just scare you off."

"But you didn't scare me off." She smiled. "So that hare was more effective than you." She walked under the sign:

Skene Mains
Farm Shop
— by Craigvenie —

Organic Produce
buy fresh here, or boxes
delivered to your door

and stepped into the shop, followed by Innes.

It was full of vegetables, fruit, herbs and fresh smells, but Mrs Sharpe wasn't there.

Innes said, "She'll be out the back, gathering parsnips or something."

Molly leant against the wall by the till, nudging a bucket of earthy potatoes with her toe. "I recognise that tattie. I dug it up myself, while I was chatting to the mysterious toad."

She pointed at another potato. "That one even looks like a toad. See, those could be bulgy eyes…"

"I wonder what happened to the toad, after he turned into that boy," said Innes. "He didn't even stay around and thank you properly after you'd saved him by giving up the chance to be free of your own curse."

Molly shrugged. "He did say thanks, very briefly, before he vanished."

"He didn't say who he was, though. Or who had cursed him, or why. He'd worked with us for days, he knew all *our* secrets, then he just whirled away without telling us anything."

Molly thought about the dark boy with the scarred head and the sand-coloured cloak. "Maybe his secrets were more dangerous than ours?"

"Or more embarrassing!" said Innes.

"I'm going to look for Mrs Sharpe." Molly walked behind the till and pushed at the back door. The gust of air as it jerked open lifted a gleaming black feather from the counter. She held out her hand and the feather drifted onto her palm. She put it in her pocket so she could use both hands to shove the stiff door further open, and walked out into the farmyard.

She checked the barns and sheds, and looked out the top-floor windows of the bunkhouse they'd stayed in last week. But she didn't spot the white-haired witch anywhere. Molly returned to the shop, where Innes was nibbling a carrot.

"I didn't see her. Maybe the curse-hatched crows scared her so much that she's left town."

Innes shook his head. "Her magic is bound to her fields, so she'd feel more vulnerable if she went too far from her farm." He opened the shop door. "We'll come back later, if your curse goes weird again."

They stepped outside.

"What are you two doing here? Buying a snack or sucking up to the witch?" A slim girl with drifting purple hair was leaning against a half-barrel planted with lavender. "You said you'd come straight back to my woods after your race. We were worried about you, weren't we, Atacama?"

A black cat slid out of the shadows by the side of the shop: a cat whose head was higher than Molly's waist, who had an almost-human face under his sharp cat ears and a pair of narrow wings folded on his sleek back.

"I wasn't worried," said the sphinx in his deep voice. "I assumed you were racing all the way to Aberlour and back."

"How did you know we were here, Beth?" asked Molly.

The purple-haired dryad smiled. "A couple of daisy fairies told me they'd seen a white stallion galloping towards the farm."

"So, Innes, who won?" asked Atacama, his long-nosed face completely serious, as if he didn't know the answer. "Who won the race this time?"

Innes sighed.

Molly grinned. "I did. But Innes won the 'becoming human at the end of the race' prize. I stayed a hare. Even when I leapt fences, walls and gates, even when I was definitely crossing a boundary from one person's land to another, I stayed a hare."

Beth turned even paler than usual. "You didn't change back? That's terrible! Did Mrs Sharpe turn you back?"

"No, we came here for advice, but I shifted at the farm gates."

"Just as well," added Innes, "because the witch isn't here."

"Mrs Sharpe's not here?" said Atacama. "Really? That's unusual at this time of day, isn't it? So... em... is anyone worried about her? Is there any sign of trouble in the shop?"

"Nope," said Innes. "She'll just be delivering cabbages to someone with a coleslaw crisis—"

"How can you *joke*?" snapped Beth. "If Molly's curse is getting worse, that's really serious. What was it like, being trapped as a hare?"

"Being a hare for a wee while is fine, so long as I don't meet a fox or a greyhound. But thinking it would never end was horrible. I didn't think I'd ever talk to you again, or eat pizza, or pick up a pencil, or use a phone. So I hope it doesn't happen again."

"There's only one way to make sure it doesn't happen again," said Beth. "Lift or break your curse."

"That's what you always say. But look, here I am, safely back to a girl again. So perhaps it's not the curse itself that's the problem, it's just not working right today. Why would that happen, Atacama?"

The sphinx sat down neatly beside her, his tail wrapped round his paws. "Curses don't usually get worse. Mrs Sharpe might know of a precedent, but I've never heard of it. I suppose the curse-caster could reword the curse to change the rules, but I doubt anyone else could. If another magic-user wanted to hurt you, they would cast a new curse."

"So you think Mr Crottel has made the curse worse? Why? I haven't annoyed him since last week."

"Whatever has happened to your curse," said Beth, "we must visit Mr Crottel and demand that he lifts it now."

"But last time I asked, Mr Crottel refused to lift it, then set his dogs on me. Asking politely won't work any better the second time around."

"Yes, it will. We'll all go with you. Mr Crottel won't want to make enemies of us all: a dryad from the woods, a kelpie from the water and a sphinx from the fabled beast community. We won't threaten him out loud, we'll just stand there looking stern, then he'll realise you have powerful friends, so he'll lift the curse and any weird changes he's made to it."

"But what if that doesn't work?"

"You could consider the ancient archaic way of breaking a curse," said Atacama, softly. "If you challenge your curse-caster to magical combat and defeat him, you break the curse."

"I didn't know you could do that," said Innes. "Why did no one tell me last week when I was trying to lift the curse on my family?"

"Because the witch's workshop was designed to make magical combat unnecessary," said Atacama, "and because Molly found ways to lift our curses in a less violent fashion. However if Mr Crottel is provoking us by making Molly's curse worse, it may become necessary."

Molly shook her head. "How could I defeat a witch in magical combat?"

"You'd have to become a witch yourself, obviously, but that's not a big step. We already know one of your ancestors was a witch."

"But I don't want to become a witch."

"You don't have to," said Beth. "We'll persuade him to lift the curse this morning." She started to walk away from the farm shop.

Molly sat down on the edge of the barrel. "I think we should wait until we can speak to Mrs Sharpe."

Beth turned round. "I think you're either a complete wimp who can't ask an old man one simple question or you actually *want* to stay cursed! Which is it?"

Molly didn't answer.

Beth grabbed Molly's arm and pulled her to her feet. "There's no such thing as a good curse. I know you sometimes like being a hare. But you live in a city! Once the October holidays are over and you're back home in Edinburgh, how could you possibly stay safe as a hare?"

Molly shrugged.

"Curses are dangerous dark magic, designed to hurt, to punish, to kill. A curse is never something to embrace or enjoy. And this one has just got worse! So you need to free yourself from it. And you need to do that *now*!"

Beth was always so calm when she was talking to her silver birch trees, so respectful of the birds and animals in her wood. But now she was standing in front of Molly with her wild purple hair tangled about her face, her silver jewellery glinting like blades on her black clothes, and her long fingers prodding painfully at Molly's shoulder.

"Stop bullying her," said Innes. "I know you have a problem with witches and dark magic, and I know you think it's harmful for Molly. But she likes being a hare, she loves beating me in races and I don't think shapeshifting does her any damage. If she can work round this new wrinkle in the terms of her curse, she'll be fine. So it's up to Molly. It's her choice."

They all looked at Molly.

"It is my choice, thank you. And of course I want to lift the curse. I'm human. I'm just human. It's not natural for me to change into a hare. Anyway, if I stop shifting now, I'll keep my perfect record of beating Innes in kelpie-versus-cursed-hare races. Racing as a hare is fun, but living as a hare is dangerous, and being stuck as a hare is terrifying. So let's see if you can glower menacingly enough at a smelly old man to force him to lift my curse."

Molly, Beth and Innes walked past Aunt Doreen's cottage, towards Mr Crottel's front gate. Atacama, who'd taken a less public route round Craigvenie, was waiting in the shadow of the distillery warehouses. He sprinted over and Beth opened the gate to let him into Mr Crottel's high-hedged garden before he could be seen by anyone driving past.

Molly took a deep breath and tried to forget how scared she'd been last time she was here. She walked up Mr Crottel's cracked path, heard the gate clang and looked round.

Her three friends were standing in a line behind her. Beth with hands on hips and face set in a scowl; Atacama with teeth bared and tail moving like a snake; Innes with crossed arms and fierce frown.

Molly laughed. "Very impressive!"

Before she stopped laughing, while she still felt protected by her friends and their put-on angry faces, she whirled round and knocked – **Rat-tat** – on the door of the man who'd cast a curse designed to kill her.

She waited. No one answered.

Molly stretched her hand forward and knocked again: **Rat-tat**.

And again, no one answered.

Molly said quietly, "He's not here."

"The dogs aren't here either," said Atacama, "or we'd have heard them inside."

"We'll come back later." Molly walked down the garden path, not sure whether the relief she felt was because she didn't have to face that nasty old man, or because she might become a hare at least one more time.

She stepped onto the pavement, watching out for the dog dirt Mr Crottel always threw there. But the pavement was clean.

"When did it last rain?" she asked Beth, who usually knew these things.

"Two nights ago."

"Then either Mr Crottel has started cleaning up his dogs' mess properly, or he and his dogs have been away since yesterday. If he's on holiday, he might not be home until after school starts again, and that'll be too late."

Molly heard a harsh noise behind her. She turned and looked at the house.

A dozen crows were perched along the roof, sharp black shapes outlined against the cloudy grey sky. One of them cawed.

"Walk away," whispered Atacama. "Don't look back."

As Molly and her friends walked away, all the crows cawed at once, *Kraa-kraa-kraa-ha-ha!*

Molly wondered if they were laughing at her, warning her, or threatening her.

Chapter Three

As they walked away from the empty house and the noisy crows, Molly asked, "Are they curse-hatched crows? Are they flocking to Mr Crottel's house because my curse just got worse? Does worsening a curse hatch out another curse-hatched crow?"

"I doubt it," said Atacama. "It's not a new curse."

"And those aren't hatchlings," said Innes. "They're adult crows. Perhaps they're just ordinary crows, nothing to do with the curse-hatched at all. Their boss, Corbie, is probably still re-growing his feathers after we defeated him last week."

"Ordinary crows are feeding at this time of day, not flocking," said Beth. "We really must lift Molly's curse and get her away from dark influences like the curse-hatched."

"I can't help until later," said Atacama. "It's nearly the start of my shift."

"We'll come with you," said Innes, "and pick your brains while you sit outside your boring closed door."

They walked quickly past the busy distillery into the

quieter yard behind the cooperage, where barrels were stored.

Molly asked Atacama, "Is this where you work?"

"The door I guard is round here." He led them between two tall pyramids of piled-up casks, to a space between the pyramids and a high stone wall.

Behind the right-hand pyramid, Molly saw a black door set in the stone wall. And she saw a slim, golden, rosette-spotted sphinx sitting in front of the door.

"You're late," said the sphinx.

Atacama sighed. "I'm not late, Caracorum, I'm exactly on time."

"You should get here early, for a handover. So 'on time' is, in fact, late."

"What is there to hand over?" he asked.

"I have nothing to report."

"There. That didn't take long. So I'm not late."

The golden sphinx stood up and stared at Molly, Beth and Innes. "Are your friends staying?"

"Not for long. They won't distract me."

"They'd better not." She stalked off, her tail in the air.

"Sisters," growled Atacama, then he sat in the perfect pose: head up, ears pricked, tail round his paws, like a statue carved from shining black rock.

Innes leant against the wall and the girls leant against the curved wood of the casks.

Atacama said in his most serious voice, "We all promised to lift each other's curses. Molly lifted ours, but we haven't lifted hers yet. So, how are we going to keep our promise?"

Beth said, "Plan A was asking Mrs Sharpe about the sudden change in Molly's curse. That didn't work because Mrs Sharpe wasn't at the farm. Plan B was asking Mr Crottel to lift the whole curse. That didn't work because Mr Crottel wasn't at home. Do we have a Plan C?"

The sphinx shrugged. "An archaic challenge probably isn't wise."

"Why not?" asked Innes.

"Because fighting with magic is unpredictable and dangerous."

"Especially when I'm not a witch," said Molly, "and I don't want to become one. I think I'd rather be a hare."

Beth frowned. "It must be possible to free you from this curse without getting you deeper into dark magic."

Atacama said, "Every potential method relies on persuading or forcing the curse-caster to lift the curse. Until Mr Crottel comes back, there's nothing we can do."

Innes added, "Until Mrs Sharpe comes back, there's no one we can ask for advice."

Molly frowned. "Is it a coincidence that both our options have vanished on the day my curse got worse? Is it a coincidence that we saw crows at Mr Crottel's house, and that I found a—"

"Your options haven't vanished completely," said a calm voice. "Let me through that door and I will show you where your options have gone."

A boy stepped out from behind the other pyramid. A tall dark-skinned boy, dressed in a white linen tunic and trousers, leather sandals and a desert-coloured cloak. But his exotic unseasonal clothes weren't the most noticeable thing about him.

Molly couldn't help staring at the grazes and scars on his head, which hadn't healed since the first and only time she'd seen him: at the end of the curse-lifting workshop when the toad had transformed into this boy.

"Let me through that door," the boy repeated, as he walked between the pyramids towards them.

Atacama said, "I can't let anyone through unless they answer my riddle."

"You know I can't answer your riddle. But if you let me through, I can find answers to the questions I half-heard as I stood in the shadows, questions about vanished curse-casters and ways to lift curses. So let me past."

Atacama stood and blocked the door. "No entry without an answer."

"Just this once. Please. To prevent any further unpleasantness."

"Unpleasantness for whom?" asked Innes. "After the last time you tried to get through this door, the most unpleasant thing that happened was you becoming a toad. And you needed a human girl to free you. So what on earth could you do that would frighten a sphinx?"

The boy smiled. "I don't want to frighten him. I don't want to frighten any of you. I just want to make a polite request and receive a positive answer. Atacama, will you please let me through that door?"

"No," said the sphinx.

"There you go, toad-boy," said Innes. "You've asked. He's answered. So leave him alone."

"I can't," said the boy. "I must get through that door." He stepped towards Atacama and raised his left hand.

The sphinx flinched, but stood firm.

Innes roared, "Leave him alone!" and turned into a horse so fast that his human voice was still echoing around the pyramids while his horse legs kicked at the boy in the cloak.

The boy whirled round, ducked under the white horse's slicing hooves and clapped his hands together.

Molly was picked up by a hot dry gust of wind. She gasped a mouthful of gritty air as she was thrown sideways, arms flailing, legs trailing.

The wind dropped her, and she slammed hard into the ground between the left-hand pyramid and the wall. Beth fell on top of her and Innes crashed down further into the dark alley.

Grains of sand pattered down around them. Then there was silence.

They pulled themselves upright and looked at the boy.

His hands were held out facing them, threatening them with another punch of air. "It's not wise to take me by surprise. Is anyone hurt?"

Beth said quietly, "We're not hurt, but that's no way to treat us. We were your friends last week."

"You weren't really my friends. You didn't know who I was." He glanced back at Atacama, standing in front of the door with teeth bared and fur spiked. "But you are the sphinx's friends. I wonder..."

He pushed his hands together, then pulled them apart, twisting and flicking them at the two girls and the horse.

Suddenly they were trapped in a cage, a rounded cage of see-through curves and rings. They all shivered as the air around them grew colder. Molly reached her hand out, but snatched it back as the pulsing cold near the curved bars burnt her fingers. They were inside a barrel of clear ice. A huge barrel, filling the width of the alley, with narrow gaps between the curved staves and round hoops.

The boy pointed at Molly, Beth and a newly human Innes. "Stay still and don't panic. I'll set you free as soon as the sphinx cooperates." He turned to Atacama. "Let me through the door and I'll let them out of that cage."

"Ignore him," yelled Innes. "We're perfectly happy in here. It's got lots of air holes. And it will either melt before teatime or I'll kick it into icicles. Don't let him near your door."

Atacama growled. "I won't. No one gets through without the answer."

The scarred boy sighed. Then he crunched his hands into fists.

The barrel started to shrink.

Innes laughed, changed into a horse and kicked the nearest bar of ice. The ice cracked. Innes kicked again and the crack lengthened.

The boy smiled. "It won't be that easy, kelpie." He drew a curved line in the air with his finger and the cracked stave of ice refroze, thicker and whiter and stronger.

Innes kicked again and again, but each time he made a crack in the slowly shrinking ice, the tall boy repaired it.

The boy said, "They can't get out, sphinx. So you have to let me in."

Atacama shook his head.

The boy's voice grew more urgent. "Please, Atacama. Your friends will freeze when that ice touches them, then be crushed as it tightens round them. *Let me through!*"

Molly moved closer to Beth and Innes, further from the painful cold of the approaching ice. Innes changed back into a boy, as the space inside the barrel reduced.

Atacama said, "I don't want you to hurt them. But I can't let you through unless you answer my riddle. So please, make an effort to answer it."

"I don't want to hurt them either. However, I can't answer your riddle. I have many powers, but the twisted logic of riddles isn't one of them."

Atacama stared at his friends in the cage of ice. "Then let's compromise, toad. If you stop that barrel closing in, I'll give you unlimited chances to answer the riddle. Hold the ice steady, don't harm my friends, and I'll let you try out answers until the end of my shift. Even a dunce like you is bound to get it right eventually."

The boy nodded and lowered his hands. The barrel stopped shrinking.

Molly sighed with relief. It was uncomfortably cold so close to the ice, but the cage wasn't actually touching any of them.

As Atacama asked his riddle, Innes whispered, "We can't let Atacama bend his rules for us. We must escape in the time Atacama's bought us, so he doesn't have to let that boy through." He held his arms out, measuring the space around him. "There's just enough room for me to shift to a horse, but I can't break these staves and hoops if that toad-boy makes the ice stronger every time I crack it. Beth, could you bring down enough wooden barrels to distract him, while I kick our way out?"

Beth shook her head. "The wood of the barrels has absorbed the liquids they've stored. They're not pure wood anymore, so I can't control them."

Molly looked up at the mountain of barrels. "I can distract him."

"How?" asked Beth. Then she looked at the small gaps between the icy curves and circles around them. "No! What if you can't change back?"

"But if he can't answer the riddle..."

They listened to the boy trying to find an answer:

"A dandelion?"

"Wrong."

"A spider?"

"Wrong."

Molly shrugged. "If he never gets it right, Atacama can't let him through, and we'll be crushed in this icy cage.

I'd rather live as a hare than die as an ice-cube. And even if I'm stuck as a hare, at least the two of you will be fine."

"No," said Beth. "You can't do that for us. Don't—"

Molly smiled, and growled, and felt the usual flash of heat down her spine as she shifted. Then she leapt through the biggest hole she could see in the frozen lattice. The tips of her ears brushed the agonising ice as she escaped from the cage.

She touched the ground once, leapt onto the lowest layer of wooden barrels and ran up the pyramid, bouncing off each curved cask, pushing herself up and up and up.

Molly wasn't used to running up such steep inclines. She knew there were mountain hares in Scotland; perhaps she was even a mountain hare herself. She must be able to do this. But it was like running up a wall, leaping almost vertically rather than horizontally.

Her front paws landed on a metal hoop on the fourth layer of barrels. The smooth metal gave her no purchase, her claws clicked and skidded, and she started to fall. But she dug her hind paws down and in, threw herself upwards and regained her balance. She kept leaping higher and higher, until she reached the sun-warmed wooden summit of the pyramid.

She looked down. To her left she could see Innes and Beth, pressed close together in the glistening cage. To her right she could see the boy, facing Atacama. He had his back to the cage, but one hand twisted behind him, pointing at the icy barrel, holding the spell steady.

Atacama was sitting calmly in front of the door, asking the riddle again, slowly, patiently, as if he was helping a small child with a reading book.

...say what you like to me,
but my face will never show any emotion.
What am I?

"A mask?"

"Wrong."

"Is it... Oh, I don't know. Give me a clue!"

"You know I can't give you a clue."

Molly moved carefully along the top of the pyramid until she was nearer the boy, nearer his bashed and bruised skull, nearer that hand trapping her friends in an icy cage.

Atacama said, "Try again. You might get it this time."

"A pair of gloves?"

Innes laughed. "You really are useless at riddles, aren't you?"

The boy glanced round at the cage. "Hey, where's Molly?"

And Molly leapt.

She flung herself off the top barrel. She hurtled down through the air. And she crash-landed on the boy's head.

He yelled in shock. His hand dropped.

Innes was already a horse, already kicking the cage to smithereens.

Molly slid down the boy's skull and landed awkwardly

on his shoulder. He reached up to grab her, but she leapt down his back and landed at his heels.

She heard the familiar thunder of Innes's hooves. She saw him emerge from the ice shards and gallop towards the boy, towards her.

The boy lifted his hands. Innes swerved out of the way and lashed out, not at the boy, but at the pyramid beside him.

Molly heard Innes's hooves **boom** against the hollow barrels. She saw the pyramid shiver and shake.

She saw a huge wooden cask falling directly towards the boy. Directly towards her own fragile hare body.

So Molly turned and ran, away from the cloaked boy, away from the shattered cage, away from the angry horse, away from the barrels rolling and thumping down the side of the pyramid.

She heard several echoing crashes and thuds. And one scream.

She skidded to a stop and turned round. There was a jagged gap in the side of the pyramid she'd just climbed. A heap of rocking barrels between the pyramids. And a pair of motionless sandals sticking out from under the heap.

Innes reared up one more time, kicking the air in triumph.

Molly ran back, as Innes shoved the empty barrels off the boy.

When Molly reached them, Innes was shifting back to his human form, Beth was brushing flakes of ice off her black clothes and Atacama was sitting in front of the door, not a smooth cat-hair out of place.

Innes said, "Good idea, Molly, using your size to escape the cage. Brave too, when we've no idea how to turn you back."

Molly looked at the boy. He was lying on the ground, not moving.

Beth knelt beside him. "He's still breathing, but those barrels knocked him out."

"Good," said Innes. "He was ungrateful, dangerous and trying to force Atacama to break his vows."

Molly moved closer to the boy. He was thin, almost gaunt, with the sharp bones in his face and hands clear under his dark skin.

Beth pointed to the boy's head, newly scarred in dozens of places, like he'd been shaved against his will. "It looks like someone attacked him."

"I attacked him," said Innes. "Very effectively too."

"No, before that. Before he was a toad. He doesn't look well. Even though he attacked us, we can't leave him lying here."

Atacama nodded. "That's the second time he's tried to force me to let him past. My family will take me off the rota again if they think I'm being targeted. I'll tidy up while you take him somewhere secure, then we can find out why he's desperate to get through this door and what he meant about answers to our questions."

Innes looked at Molly. "Your aunt's away this afternoon.

Could we take him to her house?"

Molly dipped her head down and up, in an awkward hare's nod.

"I'll join you at the Drummond cottage, as soon as my shift is over," said Atacama.

Innes changed to a horse again, Atacama and Beth draped the boy over his back, and Molly loped along beside the horse and dryad as they walked out of the cooperage yard.

As they walked past Mr Crottel's gate, on the way to Aunt Doreen's cottage, Molly stopped. She didn't want to go back into the garden where her curse had been cast, but she wondered if it might help her shift back.

Beth looked round and saw Molly crouched on the pavement. She nodded. "Witch's gateposts. Like at the farm. Clever."

The dryad pushed the gate open and Molly stepped warily through. She felt a slow fizz tickling along her spine, she lost control of her long legs and fell over. Then she felt her ears shorten and her limbs straighten.

As soon as she could stand, she staggered out of the garden. She smiled shakily at Beth. "I don't know why witches' gates work when walls and fences don't, but at least something works." She pulled the gate closed and looked up at the roof. The crows had gone.

"It took longer to work, though," said Beth. "You didn't shift in the blink of an eye, like you usually do. I actually saw your fur become skin and clothes. Did that happen at

Skene Mains too?"

"I think so."

Beth frowned at the unconscious boy on Innes's back. "Let's hope he has some answers, because we keep finding more unpleasant questions."

Chapter Four

When they reached Aunt Doreen's garden, Molly and Beth slid the cloaked boy off the horse's back and dragged him to the doorstep. Innes shifted into human form, while Molly unlocked the front door.

Molly called, "Aunt Doreen?"

There was no answer.

"She'll not be back from Elgin until teatime. Let's take him to the kitchen, it's the biggest room."

They struggled to manoeuvre the tall boy's flopping legs and sharp elbows along the narrow corridor and into the large bright kitchen built onto the back of the cottage. Then they put him down.

The boy didn't move. He just lay there, flat, on the stone-flagged floor.

Innes crouched by his head.

"He's not dead, is he?" said Beth.

Innes touched the boy's throat gently. "He still has a pulse. We'd better make him safe."

Molly looked round. "We could put him on the couch,

so he's comfy, and put cushions on the floor, so he doesn't bruise himself if he rolls off."

Innes laughed. "Not that kind of safe! I'd happily let him pick up a few more bruises. No, we need to make him safe like you make a bomb safe. We need to neutralise his magic, so he doesn't encase us in ice as soon as he wakes up."

"Could we use iron?" suggested Beth.

Innes shook his head. "Iron is for faeries." He pointed at the boy's scalp. "A forest faery would glamour something over those ugly scars."

"Running water?" Beth pointed at the sink. "We could turn the taps on."

"Running water is for evil spirits." Innes prodded the boy's shoulder. "I don't know if he's evil or not, but he's certainly solid."

"Garlic?" suggested Molly.

"He's not a vampire. We saw him standing in the daylight."

Beth said, "Will *anything* work against him? He had more power than any witch I've ever met. It didn't even feel like magic. It felt… deeper. Stronger."

"Someone turned him into a toad." Innes stood up. "And he's just been defeated by a hare and a horse. So he's not all-powerful." He looked round the kitchen at the white units, the blue range, the big dining table and the small couch by the window. "We could create a circle round him. Keep him and his magic enclosed in one safe space, so he doesn't knock the house down before we've had time to talk to him."

Beth nodded. "What would we use to mark the circle?"

"Anything that will make a clear unbroken line on the floor."

Molly thought about the contents of the kitchen cupboards. "Food colouring?"

"Too thin," said Beth.

"Flour? Sugar? Salt?"

"Sugar is too sweet, flour is too floaty," said Innes. "But salt has strength, especially sea salt."

Molly opened cupboards, searching for the container of salt crystals her aunt used to refill the salt grinder. "Here. It's heavy, so it must be nearly full."

Innes grinned. "Perfect."

Then Beth moved the wooden table and chairs nearer the cooker, and Molly dragged the boy into the middle of the clear space. As she slid him across the floor, she looked at his bashed scalp. She grabbed a stripy cushion from the couch and placed it under his head.

Innes filled a glass of water and clinked it down on the stone floor beside the cushion. "He might be thirsty when he wakes, and we can't pass things in and out of the circle."

"We should give him food too," said Beth.

Innes shook his head. "That would look like we plan to imprison him in the circle for a long time."

"Imprison him?" said Molly. "Is that what we're doing?"

"To imprison his magic, we have to imprison him as well," said Innes.

"But… that doesn't seem right. He was part of our team just a few days ago."

"I know. But we just defeated him. He'll be angry with us when he wakes up, and you saw how dangerous he was. This will keep us safe until we find out why he's trying to get past Atacama and what he knows about those vanishing witches."

"I still think we should give him food," said Beth. "He's very thin."

"He's not a baby bird or stray kitten. He's a violent powerful magic-user. But you can feed him if you want."

Beth frowned. "I suppose he did curse Atacama to lose his riddle a couple of weeks ago. If he's a curse-caster, then he misuses magic in dark and dangerous ways. I don't suppose we want to feed that…"

"Is casting curses the worst possible use of magic?" asked Molly, as she moved a chair further from the boy's feet.

"Hardly," said Innes. "I can think of much worse—"

"Totally," said Beth. "Curses are an unnatural warping of the potential of magic spells. It's the most appalling thing you can do with magic. So curse-casters are the worst magical beings possible." She looked at the boy on the floor suspiciously. "We might not be able to trust his answers, even if he does talk to us."

"Not all curse-casters are dark and untrustworthy," said Innes quietly. "Mrs Sharpe cast a curse on that wrym and you were happy to stay in her bunkhouse."

"That was different," said Beth. "We needed her workshop to lift our curses."

Innes shook his head. "That's so hypocritical. You can't say all curse-casters are bad, then say it's ok to take advice from a curse-caster when it suits you." He sighed. "Right. Let's make this circle."

As Innes paced round the room, muttering about diameter and circumference, Molly looked at the skinny boy on the floor, grabbed a packet of crisps from the nearest cupboard and dropped it beside the glass of water.

Innes crouched down and put a tiny pile of salt crystals about ten centimetres from the boy's feet, then another much further from his right knee. He went round the whole boy, dotting the outline of a circle. Then he stood on a chair, looked down and shook his head. "That pile near his left shoulder, Molly, move it closer. Good. And Beth, the one by his right ear should be further out." He asked Molly and Beth to move a few more piles, then finally nodded.

He jumped down. "Who should draw the circle? There's a lot of wooden furniture in the room – if that would enhance your power, Beth, perhaps you should create the circle?"

The dryad shook her head. "There's more metal and stone in this kitchen than wood, so I don't have much influence. You'd better do it, Innes."

"I did defeat him less than an hour ago, which might give me power over him now. Molly, stand on the chair and tell me if I go squinty."

Molly watched as Innes poured the salt in one long slow smooth curve, joining all the dots and making a perfect white circle round the unconscious boy.

As he completed the circle, joining the end of the line of crystals to the start, Molly felt a release of tension, a warming and calming of the air in the room.

"Well done," said Beth. "I felt that take. He's in there with all his power and we're out here, and that circle will keep us separate."

Molly said, "It's just a line of salt. How can it keep him in one place? It wouldn't even keep me in and I don't have any magic at all."

"Think about how powerful boundaries are for you: all those walls and gateposts you need to turn human again," said Innes. "We've made a boundary, and we can hold him inside until he's answered our questions."

"He can't answer any questions until he wakes up," said Molly. "Does anyone want a snack?"

She found smoothies and homemade biscuits for her friends, feeling slightly guilty about the water and plain crisps they'd given the boy on the floor.

When she brought the tray of snacks over, Innes and Beth were looking at a display of photos above the couch.

"That's my wood!" Beth pointed at a black-and-white photo of children in old-fashioned clothes, lined up in front of leafy trees.

Molly nodded. "Aunt Doreen says the Sunday school had a bluebell picnic there every year when she was wee."

Innes was looking at an orange-tinted group of children in flared jeans, leaning on a rough stone wall.

Molly smiled. "My dad and his friends, playing Poohsticks on the bridge near your mill-house."

"And that's you." Beth pointed at a picture of Molly laughing, between two smiling adults, in front of the Eiffel Tower.

"Last summer, with my mum and dad." Molly sighed. "They don't get much time off, so that's why I spend most school holidays up here, in Dad's old home town with Dad's old aunt."

"So why have we never met you before?" asked Beth.

"I suppose because I've never been cursed, needed magical help and attended a witch's workshop before. Anyone want a biscuit?"

"We don't take family holidays," said Beth. "The trees are our family too, so we need to stay here. It's the same for your family's rivers, isn't it, Innes?"

He nodded. "But adult kelpies go on lone hunting trips, which are like holidays. It's only safe to stalk prey far from our home rivers."

"Your mum told my Aunt Jean that your dad has gone on a hunting trip," said Beth, "to celebrate the lifting of your family's curse. Do you know where he's gone?"

Innes sat down and examined the biscuits. He carefully chose the one with the most chocolate chips and fewest raisins.

Molly sat beside him. "How far away does your dad have to travel? Is it like my mum going to London for meetings?"

"We never go as far south as London. We usually go north and west from here. But whichever direction a kelpie goes, we have to hunt outside the catchment of our own river system. So I'm sure my father is exactly where he's meant to be right now."

Beth squeezed in beside Molly and picked up a biscuit. "Those crows seemed pleased we couldn't find Mr Crottel. Do you think they know where he's gone?"

"I think Mrs Sharpe was visited by crows too," said Molly. "Innes, did you see that black feather by the till in the shop?"

Innes shook his head, his mouth full of biscuit.

Beth frowned. "I wonder if we're wasting time waiting for that boy to wake up and tell us what he meant by vanishing curse-casters. Perhaps we should go to the crows' Stone Egg Wood right now, to search for the witches or for clues. I could wait outside on guard while you both sneak in."

"We can't go out and leave a strange boy lying on my Aunt Doreen's kitchen floor."

Innes swallowed and nodded. "That could be dangerous, for her."

"Don't worry about Molly's aunt," said a calm voice. "I wouldn't hurt her. After all, she didn't knock me out. That was one of you."

They looked over and saw the boy sitting up in the centre of the circle.

"Which one of you hit me on the head?" He looked at Molly, then at Beth, then at Innes.

"We didn't hit you," said Beth. "The falling barrels hit you."

Molly stood up. "I distracted you, so Innes could attack you. I'm not going to apologise. You were threatening us and trying to force Atacama to break his vows."

Innes stood up too. "I kicked half a dozen barrels onto you. I'm not going to apologise either. You deserved it."

"Would you be quicker to apologise if I was outside this circle?"

Innes grinned. "Possibly. But I'm not letting you out until you've answered our questions. You've got water and food."

The boy took a gulp of the water, ignored the crisps and sat cross-legged on the cushion. Then he nodded. "Ask your questions."

"You know who we are," said Innes. "You spent days listening to us talk about our lives, our families and our curses. We don't know who you are."

"I am Theo."

"What are you?"

"I'm a magician."

"A stage magician?" asked Molly.

He laughed. "Did you think that ice was a theatrical effect? I'm an elemental magician. I work with the deepest levels of magic, not the superficial levels used by witches and other commonplace magic-users. They cast spells to tweak the surface of the world's magic; I manipulate the elements at a more fundamental level."

Innes crossed his arms. "If you're so deep and

fundamental, why couldn't you transform yourself back from that toad?"

"I was cursed by a being with access to even older magic than mine. She hacked off my hair to destroy all the power I'd absorbed as I trained. She wrapped a curse round me so many times that I couldn't unpick its layers on my own. Then she threw me into the air, and as I fell back to earth I changed into many different creatures. I was a toad when I hit the ground, so I was trapped as a toad. I was too weak after the attack to break the curse myself. The stone egg, the good deeds held inside it and the naïve words of the farm-witch were all necessary to crack the spell and allow me to force my way out."

"But the good deed inside the egg was a con," said Molly. "You and I tricked that flower fairy into letting us help her."

Theo smiled. "You were all helping each other, and those were genuine good deeds. Then when you asked Mrs Sharpe to lift my curse rather than yours, Molly, that generous act gave the egg even more power. All Mrs Sharpe did was crack the eggshell and say a few encouraging words. You freed me, Molly. So thank you. Thank you all.

"Thank you also, obviously, for trapping me again. And in a circle of salt crystals! It's refreshing to be held prisoner by such primitive power. Who created it?"

He stared at each of them in turn.

Innes took a deep breath. "I created the circle. And we have more questions. Why do you want to get past Atacama? What do you know about Molly's curse-caster vanishing?"

"I'm not going to tell you. Not while I'm sitting on a cold floor in an amateurish gritty circle."

"It's a perfect circle! And we gave you a cushion and food and water."

"I've finished the water and I'm not tempted by the crisps. We saw enough potatoes in the witch's muddy fields. The biscuits outside the circle look much tastier. So, I won't answer any more of your questions until you answer mine. Do you know what the sphinx guards? And what is the answer to his riddle?"

Innes laughed. "That's what you want? The answer to Atacama's riddle! You're not going to learn that from us. And you will tell us everything we want to know. Right now."

Theo smiled and put his finger on his lips.

Innes walked forward. He stood at the edge of the circle and raised his voice. "You are my prisoner, defeated by my hooves, in my circle, under my power. You will answer my questions."

"Really? You think you have *any* power over me?"

The tall thin shaven-headed boy stood up, straightened his cloak and stepped towards Innes. He took one short step from the centre of the circle to the edge. Then he took another step, long and slow and easy, over the salt and out of the circle.

Chapter Five

As Theo stepped forward out of the circle, Molly and Innes stepped back. Beth stood up.

"Sit down." Theo flicked a finger at them and a wall of air shoved them all onto the couch, then held them there.

Molly, sitting squashed between Beth and Innes, felt Beth breathe in and out deeply as if she was trying to calm herself. She felt Innes's arm muscles tense as if he was getting ready to fight. Molly resisted a sudden desire to become very small and very fast and run away.

Theo pulled a chair from against the wall and dragged it round to face the couch. He sat down and stared at them.

"Well. What do we do now?" He frowned. "I could hold you hostage again to force your sphinx friend to let me past. But if I do that, you'll argue with me and fight against me, and even though you won't win—"

"We did win, earlier today," muttered Innes.

"You're not winning now though, are you? If you fight against me, you'll delay me and perhaps force me to hurt you, which I don't want to do after the kindness you showed me when I was a toad. Anyway, we made a good team last week, so you could be useful allies again. I'll try to persuade you, then you can persuade the sphinx."

"We'll never ask Atacama to break his vows," said Innes.

"Won't you? Let's see. Now that I'm not sitting on the floor in an insulting little circle, ask your questions again. That's the best way for you to realise we should help each other."

Molly said, "My first question is: did that circle have any power over you at all?"

Innes said, "It held him for a while."

Theo smiled.

"Did it hold you?" asked Molly. "Or could you have stepped out at any time?"

"Not at *any* time." Theo grinned. "Only when it was suitably dramatic. Like when an arrogant little kelpie thought he could make demands of an elemental magician."

"I thought you said the person who attacked you took all your magic," said Innes.

"She took the power I'd absorbed and stored over many years. But even a weakened magician, only able to draw on the power around him at any one moment, is still much stronger than a kelpie or a dryad or an unfortunate human victim of a witch. So, it's a pretty circle of crystals, Innes, but it had no power over me."

He waved his hand and the tiny rocks of salt shifted on the floor, breaking up the circle and creating the outline of an open eye, then a smiley face, then a long snake, which slithered over to the kitchen units, climbed up to the porcelain sink and dissolved in the dishwater.

"Tricks and games!" said Innes. "If you just use your magic to play games, you're wasting our time."

Theo nodded. "None of us have time to waste. So ask your questions."

Beth said, "What do you know that will help us lift Molly's worsened curse?"

"Why do you keep saying Molly's curse has got worse?"

Molly shrugged, her shoulders pushing against the warm blanket of air pressing her into the couch. "I don't shift back when I cross boundaries any more. I only shift when I go between a witch's gateposts."

"A curse that has changed its rules?" Theo leant forward. "That's extremely unusual. Did the caster tell you why or how he did that?"

"We couldn't ask him. He's not at home."

Theo nodded. "A missing curse-caster. That's something I can help you with, if you help me get past Atacama."

"We will never help you get past him," said Innes, "because letting someone through without the answer would go against his nature as a sphinx."

Molly asked, "Why are you so keen to get through that door?"

Theo answered with another question. "Do you know what's behind that door? You're such close friends with the sphinx, I'm sure he's told you what he's guarding."

"He can't," said Innes. "Sphinxes don't know what they guard. They guard it with their lives, but they don't know what it is."

"Really? None of them know? He may have been misleading you. Sphinxes guard secrets, but they also keep secrets."

"You're being secretive too," said Beth. "Tell us who cursed you."

"I'm not sure. I only caught a glimpse of her and she may not have been in her true form. But she was certainly more powerful than me." He sighed. "I had my full powers when I tried to get past Atacama the first time. He didn't agree to my polite request and I didn't want to hurt him in full combat, so I defended myself when he attacked, then used a light curse to try to get past. But that didn't work, because he's very stubborn. With the front door so well guarded, I decided to break in the back door. That's when I was ambushed."

"Break in?" said Innes. "All your fancy words and tricks, but actually, you're just a thief. What are you trying to steal?"

"I'm not a thief."

"Then why were you breaking in?"

"To continue my investigation into why the curse arc is becoming unbalanced and how it's threatening the integrity of the helix of magic."

Innes frowned. "The what, and the what of the what?"

"The helix of magic is formed of many arcs – the curse

arc, the transformation arc, the temporal arc, I'm sure you know them all – and each one must be balanced or the helix starts to warp. My family maintains the stability of the helix. I noticed the curse arc becoming skewed, so I'm investigating the elemental being who regulates curses."

Molly glanced at Beth and Innes. They looked as confused as she felt.

"But what's that got to do with Atacama?" asked Beth.

"He guards the front door of the Keeper's Hall: the domain of the Promise Keeper, who maintains and regulates all curses, vows and enchantments. When you were digging potatoes and building walls to lift your curses, did your friend tell you he guards the one being who can lift any curse with the wiggle of a little finger? Did he tell you that?"

"Em… No, he didn't," said Innes.

Theo shrugged. "Sphinxes keep secrets."

"But what does this have to do with the curse-hatched and Molly and Mrs Sharpe?" asked Beth.

"Mrs Sharpe?" said Theo.

"Mrs Sharpe is missing too."

Theo sighed. "Then it's escalating."

"What's escalating?"

"You know that the best way to lift a curse, unless it has an inbuilt limit, is to persuade or force the curse-caster to relent. You learnt that much last week, didn't you?"

They all nodded.

"And who benefits from long-lasting curses?"

"You're not running another workshop," said Innes. "Just tell us!"

Theo raised an eyebrow. "Beth, Molly? Who benefits?"

"The curse-hatched," said Beth. "That's why they didn't like Mrs Sharpe's curse-lifting workshop. They benefit because every time a curse is cast, a baby curse-hatched crow hatches from a stone egg, and that crow lives for as long as the curse lasts. So a curse that lasts forever means a crow who lives forever, and a lifted curse means a dead crow."

Molly remembered crows falling to the ground as she found ways to break her friends' curses. And she remembered the baby bird she'd seen with her own curse marked on its wing.

Theo nodded. "Corbie and his crows have started manipulating the curse arc to make curses last longer. They interfered with Mrs Sharpe's workshop, and I think they're also removing curse-casters from their magical communities, so the curses become almost unbreakable."

"They're kidnapping curse-casters?" asked Innes.

Beth said, "You think Corbie and the curse-hatched have taken Mr Crottel so Molly's curse can't be lifted?"

"That's my best guess."

"Where have they taken him?" asked Innes.

"I suspect they're taking curse-casters to the midpoint of the curse arc, to the Promise Keeper's Hall, where curses are managed. I can't be sure until I get through that door."

"This Keeper, the person who controls curses, is he or

she in charge of the crows?" asked Molly. "Is the Keeper ordering Corbie to do this?"

"I believe the Keeper is female this time around. And I don't know what she's up to. There shouldn't be any contact between the curse-hatched crows and the Keeper. But whether she's ordering it, or unaware it's happening, she isn't doing her job properly. So she may need to be replaced."

"How do you replace someone like that?" asked Molly. "A job advert?"

"It's not easy. Keepers live for thousands of years. This one has only been in place for a few centuries. But if she's corrupt or incapable, she must be removed."

"Removed?" asked Beth.

"He means 'killed'," said Innes. "He wants to *kill* a hugely powerful magical being."

Theo shook his head. "I don't want to kill anyone. I want to gather information and see if I can fix whatever is twisting the curse arc. If you help me, you'll probably find your missing witches and your answers about Molly's curse. It's your choice. I'll get past that stubborn sphinx eventually, but with your help I'll get in faster and we can sort this out sooner."

He stood up, held his hands out and moved away from them. The pressure lifted from their chests. "I'm not going to throw my power around any longer. You're free to go if you wish."

"Free to go?" Innes leapt up. "This isn't your house,

toad-boy. This isn't your home town. *You* are free to go, if you want."

"Innes, don't start shouting again," said Beth. "This magician might be a curse-caster, but he understands a level of magic none of us even knew existed. We might have to work together to find Mr Crottel and anyone else who might be behind that door."

Innes frowned. "You want to ask Atacama to—"

The door swung open. A long dark shape trotted in.

"Ask me to do what?" said the sphinx. "Give you wise advice? Or bat a ball of wool about? I'm on my tea-break, so I don't have much time. Quick, tell me, what do you want me to do?"

"Tell us the truth," said Innes.

"Of course. But why is our attacker roaming free? Why haven't you contained his magic?"

"I'm not that easy to contain." Theo smiled and held out his hand to the sphinx. "I'm Theo, pleased to meet you."

Atacama just stared at him. "We've met before. When you cursed me, when you threatened my friends, and of course when you were a warty little toad." He looked at Innes. "Why are you letting him wander about the Drummond cottage like a guest?"

Innes shrugged. "We made a circle, but he escaped. Now he wants us to persuade you to let him through your door."

"He wants *what*? Has he cast a spell on you?"

"I don't do simplistic surface spells."

"No. You just curse innocent sphinxes doing their job!

If you don't have the answer, I will never let you through that door. And my friends will support me." The sphinx turned confidently to Molly, Innes and Beth. "Won't you?"

But not one of them answered him.

Chapter Six

The sphinx stared at his silent friends.

Then Beth asked, "What's behind the door, Atacama? Who are you guarding?"

"I don't know. We never know."

"None of you know?" asked Innes. "How do you get paid?"

"Our senior sphinxes negotiate the contract, so they know. But the sentry sphinxes don't know. Our loyalty is to the riddle, to the answer, to the door. So, I don't know."

"Because *he* said," Beth pointed at Theo, "that the one who maintains curses is behind your door. That you've been guarding the curse keeper."

"It's the 'Promise Keeper' actually," corrected Theo.

Atacama frowned. "Really? I didn't... That would explain... I haven't been hiding the truth from you, because I didn't know. Anyway, even if the way to lift every curse in the world lies behind my door, I still can't let anyone past. I made a vow."

Beth said quietly, "But we all made a promise, to lift each other's curses. And Molly is still cursed."

"Molly will lift her curse by confronting her curse-caster, not whoever makes curses work. We lifted everyone else's curses without knowing about this Keeper, why do you need to get in now?"

Theo said, "Because my information indicates that Molly's curse-caster is also behind that door."

Atacama shook his dark head. "Your information might be wrong, toad-boy. What proof do you have?"

"The proof of my own eyes. And yours too. I was watching that door on and off for days before our first encounter, Atacama. I saw the curse-hatched escort several guests through the door. I never saw any of the guests come out. And half a dozen of them were taken through the door while *you* were guarding it."

Atacama was pacing around, his tail starting to bristle.

Theo said, "I was intrigued, because everyone I saw go in had recently cast a curse. I tried to find out what was going on, but you wouldn't let me past. When I tried to enter through the crowgate, I was attacked and cursed."

"Serves you right. I was attacked and cursed too, by *you!*"

Theo bowed his head slightly. "I've apologised, and I'm delighted you found a way round my small curse. But I still need to get in, to see how many curse-casters are inside, to discover if they're willing guests or not, and to investigate the Keeper's involvement. While I'm inside, I can look for the witch who cast and perhaps worsened Molly's curse."

Atacama said, "You really believe Mr Crottel is behind my door?"

"It seems likely. I watched a rogue selkie who cursed a colony of puffins, three witches who cursed a family of brownies and a fungus fairy who cursed a baby dryad all go through the door. Who have you seen?"

"I can't tell you." The sphinx's ears were flat to his skull, his fluffed-up tail was swishing. "And I can't stop the crows taking someone in. Even if the guest doesn't want to go, even if the guest asks me to help them. If Corbie knows the answer, I have to let the whole party through. It's my job—"

"Atacama, what are you hiding from us?" asked Innes.

"He doesn't have to tell us," said Theo. "If he lets me in, I'll find out."

"He doesn't just have to let *you* in," said Beth. "We all have to go. You want information, but we need to help Molly find Mr Crottel. We should go in together."

Molly glanced over at Atacama, who looked like a cornered animal, miserable and hunted and confused. "I don't want to ask Atacama to break his vow... But I can't go back to Edinburgh with this curse, and there might be answers behind that door. So if Atacama can let us in without breaking his vow, I'll go."

Beth looked at Innes. "Will you come with us?"

Innes scowled. "I don't know if I believe a word this cloak-swishing magician says. And I would never force Atacama to break his vow. But we did promise we'd help

Molly lift her curse. And I'd like to know where all those curse-casters have gone. We can't just let fabled beasts and magical beings vanish."

He crouched beside Atacama. "You could let us in, but leave toad-boy outside. Then we'll see if he is telling the truth about what's behind that door. Because there *is* something going on. You have seen something or someone significant go in, haven't you?"

"I'm not permitted to reveal—"

Molly gasped. "Mrs Sharpe is missing too. Did you see her taken through your door?"

The sphinx flicked his tail.

Innes said slowly, "Atacama, tell me the truth. Did you see Mrs Sharpe go through?"

Atacama flexed his claws.

"Did she go willingly or unwillingly?"

The sphinx growled.

Molly knelt beside the sphinx. "Did she ask for help? Was she the one who asked for your help and you didn't do anything?"

Atacama snarled. "It's my job! I have to ask the riddle, and I have to let anyone with the answer past! I'm a sphinx, and that is what sphinxes do!"

He rushed out of the kitchen, and out of the cottage.

Innes said, "He let them drag Mrs Sharpe through his door, and he didn't even tell us!"

"Perhaps he did try to tell us," said Molly. "At the farm, remember, he asked about evidence that she'd gone missing?"

Innes sighed. "Mrs Sharpe helped all of us last week. If the curse-hatched are holding her prisoner, we have to get her out."

"How?" asked Theo. "Your friend is refusing to open his door."

Innes grinned. "It won't be that difficult, will it, girls?"

Molly and Beth shook their heads.

"It won't be difficult for *us*," Innes continued, "but you, toad-boy, can just wait behind the casks for us to come out again."

"You don't know anything about the Keeper's Hall or the curse arc. I can be your guide, your advisor."

"I'm not taking advice from you!" said Innes.

Beth sighed. "Stop being such a territorial animal, Innes. Theo might be useful. Molly, what do you think?"

Molly looked at Theo, who smiled at her.

"You were a perfectly nice toad," she said, "and we worked well together before, so I'm sure we can work together again."

Innes said, "How can we work with him? He cursed Atacama, attacked us and escaped from our circle. And he's been unbelievably arrogant and annoying ever since he stopped being a toad and started flicking that ridiculous cloak about."

"You don't like him," said Beth.

"Really? I'm sorry if I'm giving that impression."

"But it's possible to work with someone you don't like," said Beth. "And it's possible to change your mind about someone. I didn't like Molly when I first met her, but she's my favourite hare now!"

"It's understandable that you dislike me, Innes," said Theo smoothly. "I embarrassed you in front of your friends when I stepped out of your circle, and you're used to being in charge—"

"Innes isn't in charge!" said Beth.

"When he's a horse, he's bigger and stronger than any of you, so he acts like he's in charge. He's already threatened by Molly's speed and now he's threatened by my power."

Innes said, "I'm not threatened by you, I just don't like you. And I don't trust you."

"You don't have to like me or trust me. You can even call me toad-boy rather than Theo. But ask yourself: will I be useful? With my knowledge of the curse arc, and my small insignificant weakened powers," he flicked his fingers and a crown of tiny flames started dancing around Innes's head, "will I keep your friends safe? If you think I can be useful, let me join you."

Beth said, "Innes. Think before you answer."

Innes frowned. "Ok. You might be useful. But you're not in charge."

Theo smiled. "Of course I'm not. Shall we go?"

"You know why we must enter the Keeper's Hall, so please let us past," said Beth, as they stood in front of the sphinx and the door.

"No one is getting past me," insisted Atacama. "No one will make me break my vow. Innes, you know my vow, you were my guest at the ceremony!"

Innes nodded. "Never to let anyone past, unless they know the answer to your riddle."

"As my friend since we were kittens, you won't ask me to break that vow."

"Of course I won't ask you to break that vow. But you don't have to break it to let us in. Because we already know the answer to your riddle!"

Atacama hissed.

Innes smiled. "When we helped you make up your new riddle, after toad-boy cursed you to lose the old one, you had to tell us the answer."

"But you promised never to tell anyone else that answer."

"We're not going tell 'anyone else'. We're going to tell *you*. Then you can let us all in, including this fancy flashy fool here."

Atacama shook his head.

"Ask your riddle," said Beth gently.

"No!" Atacama moaned. "If I let you in, without the right token in your hand, you'll die."

"Why? We know the right answer."

"The answer is not enough. A sphinx is a sentry. But no one employs a sphinx outside a door without another guard inside, or there's no defence against those with genuine riddling skills. There's something behind that door that will kill you if you don't show the token it requires. Please don't go in, or you will never come out."

"But if you don't know what you guard," asked Molly, "how do you know there's something dangerous in there?"

"I've never seen it, but I've heard rattling noises, then screaming, then silence."

Molly sighed. "Perhaps we shouldn't go in. I can't put you all in danger, just to help me lift my curse."

Theo said, "This isn't just about your curse, this is about all the other curse victims with no way to lift their curses while their curse-casters are missing. But that's my job, not yours. So I'll go myself, if one of you gives me the answer to Atacama's riddle. No one else has to take the risk of meeting what's behind this door."

Beth said, "I have to go too, to free Molly from dark magic forever."

Innes nodded. "I don't mind a few risks to keep a promise, and to see what the crows are up to with those curse-casters."

Molly said, "If it will help other curse victims, of course I'll go."

Atacama's ears drooped. "Please don't go in. You're my friends. I don't want to sit out here and listen to you start screaming. Then, even worse, listen to you stop screaming…"

But they all took one step closer to the door.

Chapter Seven

"If we don't go through your door," said Beth, "then we're giving up on Molly. And I'm not giving up on her. So I'm sorry, Atacama, but you really do have to ask us your riddle."

Atacama sank onto his belly. Then he spoke, softly and slowly:

I tock all day, but I never say hello;
I move my hands all day, but I never wave goodbye;
You can say what you like to me,
but my face will never show any emotion.
What am I?

Beth looked at Molly. "Theo's doing his job, Innes and I are keeping a promise, but you're taking responsibility for lifting your own curse. You should answer."

Molly took a full breath, to speak loudly and clearly. Then she glanced at Theo, leaning forward, eager to hear the solution. So she knelt beside Atacama and whispered,

"A clock," in his ear, feeling the silky tips of his black fur stroke her cheek.

Atacama nodded sadly. "You may pass."

He edged back from the door. "It's open. Just push."

Molly stood up and the others joined her. They reached out together, pushed the door open, and saw absolute black beyond.

Atacama whispered, "Goodbye."

They stepped inside and stood still, looking forwards into the dark. The soft light of the Speyside afternoon floated through the open door behind them.

The door closed with painful slowness and they stood in perfect darkness. Then the darkness began to glow.

Torches flickered into flame at head-height on the walls around them. Molly saw a corridor of white stone decorated with small tiles in simple geometric patterns.

"Mosaics," she murmured.

"They're beautiful," said Beth, reaching towards a blue-and-gold design of interlocking angles.

Theo whispered, "Don't touch! Let's get moving..."

As they walked along the corridor, the mosaics on the walls and floor became more complex: swooping wreaths of flowers and fruit, dolphins leaping in pools of water.

After another few steps, the mosaics showed stern-faced men marching, with eyes made of jewels, faces and hands made of coloured tiles, swords and spears made of shining metallic squares.

"Come on," said Theo, "faster!"

Molly heard a CLICKING sound.

Then she saw that the floor ahead sloped sharply upwards.

No. That wasn't what she was seeing. The floor was flat.

The mosaics were rising up to meet them.

Warriors created from fragments of glass and stone were lifting off the floor. Their sandaled feet stayed on the ground, but their legs and bellies and heads, their arms and hands and swords, were rising. Squares and rectangles of colour rattled as they moved upwards, then hovered in the air, blocking the corridor.

They were joined by more mosaic men, breaking away from the walls on either side.

The tall soldier in the middle, wearing a golden breastplate, with skin of terracotta tiles and eyes of green stone, spoke in a staccato voice: "Do you wish to enter the Keeper's Hall?"

"Yes," said Molly.

"Do you have the token?"

"We know the answer to the sphinx's riddle."

"Anyone can answer a riddle. Only those with the token may pass."

He thumped the butt of his spear on the floor. It clanged solidly, even though Molly could see it was made of unconnected brown and silver tiles.

"Show me the token or suffer the fate of trespassers."

"Do you have the token?" Molly whispered to Theo.

"I don't know what token they want."

Molly pulled a one pound coin from her back pocket. "I have, em, a golden token."

The mosaic man shook his head. It clinked.

"I have a smooth river pebble," Innes held a white stone on the palm of his hand, "which would fit nicely into that gap in your friend's kneecap."

The mosaic man shook his head again.

Molly dug around in her pockets. "I have—"

"Stop guessing, children. You either have the Keeper's token or you don't."

"They don't have the token," said the mosaic man to his right.

"They don't have the token," all the mosaic men echoed.

"Prepare to slice them up," said the leader.

Each mosaic man raised a weapon: a sword or spear or double-headed axe.

Molly could see the gaps between each tile. She could see right through the soldiers and their weapons. But she could also see how each tile stayed perfectly aligned to its neighbours, like birds in a flock.

"Turn and leave," said the tallest mosaic man. "Or we will slice you so small that we could use slivers of your bones as tesserae for our next wall of recruits."

"Won't those blades fall apart if they hit us?" said Innes. "Seeing as they're made of tiles held together by... nothing?" He stepped forward. "Your rickety rattling weapons don't scare me. Let us past."

The leader slashed out with his spear.

And the blade, composed of a dozen silvery tiles and a whole lot of empty space, cut a clean slit through the kelpie's shirtsleeve.

Innes nodded. "Fair enough. That's only a little bit impossible. But quite effective." He took an unhurried step back.

Beth whispered, "Innes, can you kick them to pieces?"

"I can't use hooves. Fighting in this tight space, I might kick you lot instead."

"Then how do we get past?"

"Like this." Theo held out his arms. A black shield appeared in his right hand and a dark metal sword in his left.

"Where did you get those?" asked Innes, as the mosaic men muttered amongst themselves.

"I imagined them," said Theo.

"Oh, great. Imaginary swords against impossible ones."

"I can imagine weapons for you too, if you give me permission to draw energy from your bodies."

"What?"

"We don't seem to be anywhere earthbound, so I can't draw power from the land, and I have no stored power just now. So if you want a weapon, Innes, give me permission to make one from your own life-force."

The mosaic men stepped forward, clattering on the floor.

"I need your permission," murmured Theo. "I won't do it without consent."

The mosaic men stepped closer, their blades pointing at throats and eyes.

"Yes!" said Molly. "I give you permission!"

She felt a cold ripple across her skin, and suddenly she was holding a brown shield and a sword.

"I give you permission," said Beth, and she had weapons too, purple and silver.

"Alright, go on then," said Innes, and he was holding a white shield and pale sword.

"Anyone know how to use these?" asked Molly, feeling safer behind the shield, but awkward holding the sword.

"Block with the shield, attack with the sword," said Theo, "and do it fast. If I draw power from you for too long, you'll weaken, then die."

"Weaken then die?" said Innes. "Thanks for telling us the small print beforehand."

The kelpie lunged forward and thrust his sword at the nearest mosaic man. The sword went right through the tiles, but when Innes pulled the blade out, the tiles just slid back into place.

The warrior slashed down at Innes, who lifted his shield and leapt back.

"How does this sword help?" he yelled at Theo. "How does making holes in them help, when they're mostly made of holes?"

Molly said, "You hit his armour. Try hitting their skin."

She jabbed at a mosaic man's bare upper arm. Her blade passed through with a gentle clinking sound like a wind-chime, and the warrior grinned.

"Your blades can't defeat us," said the leader. "We're

made of broken tile, broken stone, broken glass. You can't break us further."

Theo laughed. "Of course!" His sword and shield vanished. "Cover me! I have an idea."

Theo crouched down and the others surrounded him with their shields. The mosaic men attacked, slamming their impossible blades against the barrier. Theo put his hands on the floor and hissed in frustration. "There is *no* power here. Beth, can I drain more of your life-force?"

"Why?"

"As a tree spirit, your primary power is growth and repair. That's exactly what we need to defeat these soldiers. Do I have your permission?"

"Yes!"

Theo grabbed Beth's hand and she fell to the floor, her sword and shield gone. Molly and Innes leant over them, locked their shields together and braced their bodies underneath, to withstand the crashing blows of the mosaic men's blades.

As the mosaic men hacked down, Molly's arms buckled and her shield started to splinter.

Then Theo held his hand out past the shields.

Molly heard tinkling, clattering and brief screams.

She peered round the edge of her shield. The shapes of the mosaic men were being ripped apart, their eyes and faces and weapons flying in different directions. She saw all the golden tiles melting together, all the terracotta squidging together, all the glass fragments clicking together like a high-speed jigsaw.

She watched all the tiny tiles that had made up the mosaic men re-form into their original objects: a sheet of gold, a lump of clay, a mirror, a blue necklace...

There was silence.

The shield Molly was holding vanished.

"We couldn't break them further," said Theo. "But we could join their broken pieces together again."

Innes and Molly pulled Beth up. The dryad was cold and shaking. Theo was shivering too, as he struggled to his feet without help.

"What did you do to Beth?" demanded Innes.

"I used her power to work my magic. Most magicians store power and can work in any environment. I lost my stored power when I lost my hair, so I can only use what's around me. Normally that's the ground under my feet, but here there's only the three of you. And Beth's power was the best fit for my magical purpose this time, so I used her life-force to save all our lives."

Beth looked at the clay and the mirror. "Are the mosaic men dead? Did you kill them? Did I kill them?"

"They were just pictures with a simple magical instruction to attack trespassers," said Theo. "They weren't alive. Not like you're alive or a tree is alive. You didn't kill anything, Beth. And if anyone wants to recreate the mosaics, the materials are right here. Now let's find the Hall."

Molly, Innes and Beth walked close together, keeping their distance from the boy in the cloak. The corridor led them to a big arched wooden door, unguarded and ajar.

Beth stumbled forward and placed her hand on the door. "Old pine, but strong. I can feel the wind and the snows..." After a few moments touching the planks, she stood straight and confident again.

All four of them walked out into a clear blue morning.

They'd stepped through a doorway on the side of a tower, onto the wide wall of a white castle built on a mountain. Molly looked round. The wall formed a square, with a tower at each corner. Three towers were the same height, but the tower diagonally opposite them was several stories higher. She saw a handful of crows circle the highest tower and swoop through a window.

On both sides of the walkway along the top of the wall, the stonework had those up-and-down edges that Molly had always associated with fairytale castles. She joined Innes peering through the outer parapet. The castle was built on a broad summit, with cliffs each side and the rocky peaks of other mountains all around.

"This isn't Speyside," said Innes. "Where are we?"

They all looked at Theo, who was gulping deep breaths of the fresh air. "We are at the Keeper's Hall."

"But *where* are we? Where is the Keeper's Hall?"

Theo shrugged. "If I knew that, I wouldn't have to mess around with sphinxes in Scotland. It could be the Atlas Mountains or the Urals or the Andes. It could be anywhere.

Wherever it is, it's inaccessible, except through the door Atacama guards and the crowgate. But we've found it. Shall we look around together?"

Beth said, "If you promise not to use us as spare batteries for your fancy magic."

Innes nodded. "You're like a magical vampire, sucking our energy."

Theo sighed. "You still insult me, after I saved your lives. You're not even slightly grateful, are you?"

"We are grateful," said Innes. "We're also a bit freaked out."

Beth said, "Let's search for Mr Crottel. If we get separated, let's meet here, at the door leading back home."

Molly glanced behind her and saw the big solid wooden door fade away. She blinked. There was definitely no door, just straight lines of white stone. She pointed at the blank wall. "Our way home just disappeared."

Theo frowned. "So, as well as finding the missing curse-casters and discovering what the Keeper is up to, we'll have to search for an exit, or we'll be trapped here forever."

Chapter Eight

"So, Theo, where will we find Mrs Sharpe and Mr Crottel?" asked Molly.

Theo shrugged. "I've never been here before."

"You said you could guide us!" snapped Innes. "What was the point in bringing you, if you don't know where we should look?"

"I also said I could protect you, and I did that in the corridor."

Molly said, "Shh... I hear music. Down there."

They looked over the inner parapet to the courtyard below. A pale person wrapped round a harp was playing four slow notes, then drifting into silence, then playing the same four notes and drifting off again...

The harpist wasn't alone in the courtyard. Amongst couches, pools of water and small potted trees, Molly saw dozens of fabled beasts and magical beings, including:

A boy pirouetting slowly on delicate deer's legs
A girl with ivy in her hair

A giant lying on an enormous beanbag

A multi-coloured goat, nibbling the giant's vest

A white-haired mermaid

A scarred man in a sealskin cloak

A black-legged faun

And a familiar witch in a wrinkled three-piece suit, with his two smelly dogs.

All of them moving dreamily or snoozing.

Many of them were also eating, because the centre of the courtyard was filled with an enormous table, shaped like the spokes of a wheel without a rim, each spoke covered in white tablecloths and piles of brightly coloured foods.

The food looked tempting. But then Molly noticed dozens of crows circling the courtyard above the guests' heads, and decided she'd rather be hungry than join a feast patrolled by those dark birds.

She heard a giggle. On the other side of the courtyard, she saw a small silver-haired woman in a striped blue dress and a white apron, holding a plump baby. The baby was giggling and grabbing at a couple of golden flower fairies, who were hovering dozily just out of reach.

The woman laughed and pulled the baby back just before her chubby white hand snatched a fairy out of the air. As the woman turned to watch the fairies float away across the courtyard, Molly ducked out of sight. Everyone else was already crouched behind the parapet.

Beth said, "We've found Mr Crottel and his horrible dogs. And they're not prisoners. They look quite happy."

"They are prisoners," said Innes. "They're definitely guarded. Didn't you see the crows?"

"But where's Mrs Sharpe?" asked Beth.

"I know where she might be, if she's not a willing guest," said Theo. "I saw barred windows at the base of the highest tower."

They twisted round and looked over the parapet. At the bottom of the tower Molly saw small windows criss-crossed with dark lines.

She heard a squeal and glanced into the courtyard. The woman and the baby were getting up and leaving.

The baby was yelling "NO NO NO!" but her silver-haired granny or nanny or childminder said loudly, "Who's getting silly with the pretty dandelion fairies? You know you can't eat the guests' food and you know it's not polite to throw custard. Time for a nice nap."

The baby screamed and wriggled, working up to a serious tantrum, as the old lady carried her out of the courtyard, leaving one of the golden fairies perched on a fountain, slowly washing his wings.

Then, on the white wall behind the fountain, Molly saw a door appear.

The blank wall shimmered, and suddenly an arched wooden door was crashing open. A tall dark man in a long black coat, with one fringed sleeve shorter than the other, burst through the doorway.

"Corbie!" whispered Innes. "His feathers haven't grown back yet."

Corbie yelled, "Curse-hatched, to me!"

As the door behind him disappeared, crows flew from all round the courtyard to land at Corbie's shiny booted feet.

"The mosaic men have been defeated. We have intruders. We must search the Hall." He lowered his voice and started giving orders to individual crows.

Molly, Innes, Beth and Theo crouched behind the parapet.

Innes said, "They know we're here."

Beth said, "That's the bad news. The good news is the door might reappear anywhere. So we can search for our way out and Mrs Sharpe at the same time. Let's start at the tower with barred windows."

Molly said, "I saw a few crows flying in the top of that tower."

Theo looked up. "That must be where the crowgate opens."

"Even if the place is crawling with crows," said Innes, "we need to find Mrs Sharpe."

They crept along the battlements, staying below the lowest stones of the parapet. Molly knew that any bird flying above would spot them immediately. But the crows were still cawing and flapping in the courtyard when they reached the door to the tallest tower and stumbled gratefully into the covered darkness.

They walked cautiously down the winding staircase, passing a wooden door every few steps. Innes pushed one open and peered inside. "A bedroom," he whispered. "Probably for one of the guests in the courtyard."

Molly opened the next door. It was also a bedroom, with half a dozen tiny beds. The room after that contained one massive bed with specially strengthened metal legs.

"Fairies and giants," said Beth. "Beds for everyone."

"It's a comfy prison, but it's still a prison," said Innes. "I wonder if they knew they'd end up here, when they cast their curses?"

As they went further downstairs, the music from the courtyard got louder. Then they heard Corbie's sharp voice coming through the windows at the bottom of the tower. They all stopped.

The leader of the curse-hatched was asking: "Did you find anything in that initial sweep of the grounds?"

He was answered by a chorus of squawks.

"Nothing? Then Grasp's team will search for intruders, starting at the east tower and working round. Flock's team will watch for the door and guard it when it appears."

A high-pitched voice asked, "Should we get the guests to help search?"

Corbie laughed. "Those overfed idiots are too dopey to be any help."

Molly stood still, waiting until the sound of boot heels and wingbeats faded away. Then they all crept slowly downwards again. The stairs ended in a big shadowy room with four barred windows, two closed wooden doors, an archway into the bright courtyard, and lots of circular metal cages.

"More lucky guests," said a croaky voice, "parading past from your fancy bedrooms to your scrumptious feast, looking at us starving in our damp cages, reminding you where you'll end up if you ask awkward questions."

"They aren't guests," said a clear voice. "They're trespassers. And I'm delighted to see them."

Molly looked at the cage in the darkest corner. "Mrs Sharpe?"

The missing witch stepped closer to the bars, smiling but crumpled, her hair dusty and uncombed. "Molly, Innes, Beth and my young friend the toad. Why are you here?"

"To find you," said Innes.

"To help you," said Molly.

"To find the witch who cursed Molly," said Beth.

"To find out why the Keeper's Hall is filled with curse-casters," said Theo.

Mrs Sharpe glanced at the archway, then spoke quickly. "The curse-hatched are protecting the curses that keep them alive. The crows are bringing curse-casters here so they can't be persuaded or forced to lift their curses."

"Does the Keeper know about this?" asked Theo. "Is the Keeper behind it?"

"How do we get you out?" asked Molly.

"How do we get the curse-casters out?" asked Innes.

"Why are *you* here?" asked Beth. "Is it so you can't give advice to people trying to lift curses?"

Mrs Sharpe covered her face. "Too many questions! I can't answer them all."

"You'd better answer that last one," whispered a voice from the neighbouring cage. "These innocent little victims should know whose advice they're—"

"Hush, Morgan," said Mrs Sharpe. "That's not as important as getting everyone out."

She looked up. "If you release the guests in the courtyard, they might be grateful enough to you that they lift their curses. We've refused to join the feast, so we're locked in these cells. If you want to free us, you'll need to find the keys."

"But what about the last question?" asked Beth. "Mrs Sharpe, why have the crows taken you, as well as all these curse-casters?"

The witch looked straight at the dryad. "I think you can guess the answer."

Beth shook her head.

Innes said calmly, "You've cast other curses. Not just the wyrm round your old farm, but more curses the crows don't want you to lift."

Mrs Sharpe nodded.

Beth gasped. "Mrs Sharpe! Are there still victims suffering from your curses?"

"It's not that simple—"

There was a flash of shining wings at the bright archway, followed by a screech, *Kraa-brr!*

Mrs Sharpe called, "Get out, now! Don't worry about us. We've brought this on ourselves."

Beth opened a wooden door and looked down a white corridor. "Come on! Run!"

As Molly and the boys followed her, they heard Corbie screaming in the distance. "The intruders are at the cages!"

But the intruders were already running away from the cages.

"Where are we running to?" asked Innes.

"Just run," yelled Beth. "Don't let them separate us. That door will reappear somewhere, and we need to be ready to escape when it does. So *run!*"

They ran, with one squawking crow flying after them.

They sprinted down a corridor built along one side of the courtyard, with open arched windows looking out onto the feast. Individual crows flew through the arches and attacked them, with claws, beaks and piercing shrieks.

"They're only crows," yelled Innes. "They can't stop us running."

"They can hurt us though," muttered Molly, as a claw scraped her scalp.

They crashed through another door, into a large room with mirrors lying on a long table and propped in racks on the floor, slim vases on high shelves and jewelled chains hanging from hooks on the ceiling.

As they ran past the white table, Molly saw small

moving figures reflected in the mirrors' surfaces. In one wooden-framed mirror, she glimpsed a familiar figure standing beside a pile of dog dirt. She stopped to get a closer look, but Innes shoved her between the shoulder blades.

"Keep going!"

She ran on, through the room, into another corridor. They now had a crowd of crows above them, beating their heads and shoulders with wings. There were footsteps behind them. And the corridor ahead was blocked by men and women in dark coats with fringes dangling from the seams of their sleeves.

Theo slid to a stop. "Human curse-hatched," he gasped. "They've absorbed enough power from their curses to shift shape."

The four intruders were trapped between two groups of human curse-hatched, who were walking toward them with open arms and wide grins.

"Into the courtyard!" Innes scrambled onto the frame of the arched window.

He climbed through, followed by Beth, then Theo.

Molly was nearest the wall, furthest from the arches. By the time she took six steps across the corridor and clambered onto the sill, the curse-hatched had reached her.

She felt bony fingers grab her wrist.

Molly tried to pull away, but strong arms wrapped round her. She jabbed her elbows back, but she was dragged off the windowsill.

The woman holding her screeched, "I've got the human girl!"

Beth, Innes and Theo were still being dive-bombed by crows as they ran past a fountain. They stopped and looked back at Molly in the fringed arms of the curse-hatched woman.

Molly yelled, "*Run!* Just leave me, and *run!*" But she wasn't sure she meant it.

Beth nodded. "Follow if you can. As fast as you like."

She turned away, the boys turning with her. They ran off across the courtyard.

Molly watched as her friends left her behind, in the hard hands of the curse-hatched.

Chapter Nine

Molly struggled. The curse-hatched woman laughed and gripped tighter with clawed fingers.

Then Molly realised that Beth hadn't just run off and left her. Beth had given her instructions. *Follow. Fast.*

Molly grinned.

Molly growled.

Molly shifted.

And as a slender hare, she slipped easily out of the encircling arms.

She leapt onto the windowsill, bounced into the courtyard and sprinted after her friends. She overtook them, then slowed her pace to run beside Beth, who muttered, "I suppose your curse *is* useful sometimes."

Molly's wide vision showed more fabled beasts and magical beings in the courtyard than she'd seen from high on the walls: a glittering snake with folded wings, three white mice with silver crowns, a shining crystal hare who flicked his ears at her...

Then she hurdled a pile of smelly fur and heard a familiar sneering voice.

"You followed me, foolish girl!" said Mr Crottel. "Now you're being followed! Claw and peck her, crows, rip and tear her!"

Molly sprinted away from him. But a line of men with fringed sleeves blocked the archway ahead, so the friends turned and ran back across the courtyard.

Now Mr Crottel was fiddling with a black rose in his lapel and boasting to the mermaid in the pool beside him. "That hare is *my* curse. The crows invited me to this splendid feast when I promised to make her curse worse. They even showed me how. So that hare is my ticket to all this lovely food!"

As they ran round the courtyard, he started to sing. *"Run rabbit, run rabbit, run run run."* He prodded his sleeping dogs. "Chase her!" But the dogs just snored.

More and more curse-hatched crows mobbed the runners.

"We're too exposed," shouted Theo. He led them to a smaller archway, so low and narrow that the whole flock couldn't follow at once.

They ran into another long room and Innes slammed the door, shutting most of the crows out. They ran through that room, into another corridor, round another corner. Molly's paws skidded on the polished marble floor. Innes kept slamming doors behind them, losing more crow followers each time.

Then they ran into the room filled with mirrors again, and Innes closed the door on the last of the chasing crows.

"Are we going round in circles?" shouted Theo, as they sprinted past the table.

They heard Corbie screeching in the distance, "Catch them!"

They ran out of the mirror room and Innes shouted, "If we keep running this fast, we won't see the exit appear!"

"Does anyone have a better idea?" Beth yelled, as she led them round yet another white marble corner.

"I have an idea," said a soft voice behind them. "I could hide you."

The white-aproned, silver-haired woman stood by an open door just past the corner they'd hurtled round. They ran back towards her and she ushered them into a big bright room full of toys.

"Shh, don't wake the sleeping babe…"

But as the door closed, the baby sat up in her cot in the middle of the room.

The baby was shining. Her gold curls shone like sunbeams, her bright blue eyes reflected light like gems on a necklace and her pure white skin gleamed like it had been polished.

She opened her mouth, showing two pearl teeth, shouted, "BUNNY!" and pointed at Molly.

"Hide," said the woman. "Hide *now*!"

But the baby was crying, "Bunny bunny bunny!"

The old woman scooped Molly up. "Here, my lovely, cuddle the big bunny..." She dropped Molly into the baby's arms. "The rest of you, hide!"

Molly, held in fingers that seemed colder and harder and stronger than a baby's fingers should be, watched Innes transform into a horse and hide amongst a herd of life-sized rocking horses. Beth slid behind a tower of large wooden building blocks. Theo jumped into a ball-pit and burrowed under the blue and purple balls.

The door slammed open.

"Shhh, Corbie. The baby's in her cot!"

"My apologies, Nan. We're looking for intruders."

"There's nothing in here but me, the baby and her toys. Look round if you want, but leave the birds outside. Those feathers get everywhere."

Molly saw Corbie glance at the toys. Then he turned to the baby's cot and looked straight at Molly.

"That's right, little one," said Nan. "You cuddle your bunny."

"Bunny!" The baby squeezed Molly and rubbed her heavy hand the wrong way up Molly's spine.

Molly wanted to wriggle out of the baby's hands, to leap and run. She wanted her safety to be reliant on her own speed, not on whether Corbie would believe she was a cuddly toy. But she forced herself to stay still.

"Bunny," said the baby and held Molly up to Corbie. Molly dangled, limp and floppy.

"Is that new?" asked Corbie.

"New and fluffy!" said Nan cheerfully. "It's useful to have new friends, when teddy's in the wash, isn't it?"

The baby pulled Molly back to her tummy and squeezed tight.

"Who are you searching for, Corbie?" asked Nan, as she folded a purple blanket.

"The children who were on that curse workshop last week. I suspect they've come to free our guests."

"The Keeper won't like that. Will you, little one?" Nan patted the baby's gold curls. The curls didn't move like hair. They bounced stiffly like metal springs. "My little Keeper likes the Hall full of people to play with. Off you go, Corbie, and play hide and seek with your birds. We'll play peekaboo!"

"Peekaboo!" The baby lifted her hands from Molly to cover her face.

Molly stayed still, balanced on the baby's cold hard knees. She was desperate to run away, especially now she suspected she was being cuddled by a powerful magical being, rather than an ordinary baby. But she stayed still.

"Peekaboo!" said Nan. "I wonder where the baby is?"

Corbie sighed and turned away. "I'll let you know when we find them."

"That would be lovely, dear... Peekaboo!"

The door closed behind Corbie.

Molly was about to jump out of the cot when the baby grabbed her again. "Bunny!" The baby snuzzled her face into Molly's back.

Nan said, "Remember little things get squashed if you cuddle too tight."

The baby loosened her grip and Molly leapt out of the cot, landing at Beth's feet.

The dryad picked the hare up and held her gently. "It's ok, Molly. It's ok. That looked a bit terrifying."

Molly couldn't respond. She was stuck as a hare.

"Don't worry, Molly, we'll find a way to shift you back." Innes stepped out from the herd of rocking horses.

Theo clambered out of the ball-pit, knocking dozens of balls over the edge, and nodded to Nan. "Thank you for hiding us."

"It's nice to have lots of children in the playroom." Nan smiled. "But now we should get you home."

"That's all we want," said Beth, "to go home."

"And to discover why the curse-hatched are bringing curse-casters here," said Theo.

"And to get Molly's curse-caster out of here," Beth added.

"And everyone else, because they are sort of prisoners," said Innes.

"And to find out if the Keeper knows what's going on," said Theo.

"Look at her," said Nan. "She's just a little thing. She doesn't even know a rabbit from a hare yet, despite your friend's long ears and legs."

"I hadn't realised that Keepers grew up so slowly," said Theo, picking up a blue ball and lobbing it into the ball-pit. "Is that why the curse-hatched are becoming so powerful? Because the Keeper's too young to stop them?"

Innes picked up two purple balls and threw them into the pit.

"I wouldn't know about that," said Nan. "I'm just here to feed her, change her nappy and keep her happy. But I know she likes the Hall being full of guests. So I can get you out of here, because I know the door will be opening right there," she pointed at the wall behind the ball-pit, "in about five minutes. But I can't help you get the curse-casters out, not when they make this little one smile."

Theo moved swiftly to pick up a ball before Innes reached it, then threw it over the kelpie's head, straight into the ball-pit. He said, "But the crows bringing casters here is skewing the balance of the curse arc—"

"I don't know about balance, I only know about my little Keeper's happiness."

The boys started to race each other round the room, grabbing escaped balls and throwing them in the pit. The baby laughed at them.

Beth said, "But Nan... Is it ok if I call you Nan?"

"Nan is fine, dear. That's what they've called me for a long time. No one uses my real name now."

"But Nan, think how crowded the Hall will get, if they keep bringing curse-casters in. Think how noisy it will be and how hard it will be for the Keeper to nap. If we take them away, you'll have peace and quiet."

"It is a bit noisy, with that girl's harp and the giant's snores. Perhaps you're right." She frowned. "But the Keeper would miss them..."

Molly had a sudden idea, which she couldn't say out loud. So she wriggled out of Beth's arms and leapt over to the ball-pit, then to the stack of wooden bricks.

"What are you doing, Molly?" asked Innes. "Just let us tidy up. I've thrown in seventeen to his twelve so far." Innes narrowly missed Theo's nose with a volley of balls.

Molly ran past an old-fashioned bath and a box of cuddly toys, then bounced up and down under a shelf of beautifully dressed dolls.

"Hares don't play with toys," said Innes. "Oh, hold on. Toys! Good idea, Molly." He turned to Nan. "What if we brought the baby another toy to play with? Something to keep her happy so she doesn't miss her guests. Could we take the curse-casters away then?" He ducked as Theo threw the last purple ball into the pit.

"What a kind idea," said Nan. "I like to give her the best toys. The one toy I've never been able to get for her is the first toy, from the start of time."

"What toy is that?" asked Theo.

"A rainbow-maker, made by the first snake, who was also the first rainbow, for her first babies. A pretty rainbow made by an ancient rainbow-maker would distract this little babe while you let the casters go. So I promise you, hare and tree and horse and desert magician, if you bring the first toy here, I will show you the exit from this Hall.

Not just today, but any day, with any curse-casters you persuade to go with you." Molly thought the little old lady looked briefly taller and younger, as Nan continued solemnly, "That is a binding promise, because you have my word in the presence of the Promise Keeper."

The baby giggled. "Pro... miss."

Theo nodded. "You have my word that I will bring the first toy."

Beth said, "We will all bring it."

"But we can't find it until we get out of here," said Innes.

Nan nodded. "The door will appear any moment."

She pointed at the wall, which was painted with a mural of unfamiliar stars. They turned to look.

Nothing happened.

As they watched the smooth unmoving wall, Theo asked casually, "So does someone else do the Keeper's job just now, while she's a baby?"

"Oh no. She loves making sure people keep their promises. That's what curses are, aren't they, my poppet? Dark promises. She visits the mirrors every day between nap and lunch, to watch curses, to keep them strong, to make sure they work on time, even to lift them sometimes, when the rules have been followed and the promises have been kept."

The baby said, "Pro... miss," and started to suck her thumb.

"Does she decide on her own?" asked Theo.

"We all help her. Whoever's around makes little suggestions."

Theo frowned. "Does Corbie help?"

"The crows have been around a lot recently, chatting about promises, giving advice about curses. Do you think that's wrong?" She smiled up at Theo, wrinkles crinkling round her brown eyes. "Oh, here's the door..." She snapped her fingers and pointed at the wall again.

The door appeared.

"Hurry, it won't stay long! Good luck chasing the rainbow!"

They ran round the ball-pit, Beth pulled the door open and they all sprinted through.

As Molly bounded through the doorway, she heard the baby call, "Bye bye bunny!"

Chapter Ten

Molly leapt, in her hare form, past piles of clay and glass and other mosaic materials, then Innes hauled the outside door open and all five of them burst into the gentle light of a Speyside evening.

Where they found a weeping sphinx.

Atacama was lying down, his head on his paws, tears sliding down his dark face.

"Hey, Atacama," said Innes. "Did someone stand on your tail?"

"Innes!" The sphinx leapt up. "Beth! Molly! You're alright! I thought you were dead. I heard the clattering, the screaming, then the silence. I *knew* you were dead. And I knew it was my fault."

"It wasn't your fault." Beth knelt down and gave the sphinx a hug. "Nothing that happened behind that door was your fault. It was our fault for forcing you to let us past. Sorry."

Molly was crouched on the gravel, feeling a warm slow fizzing in her spine, ribcage and skull. She saw her paws growing, widening, flattening. The fizzing in her bones changed to a sick liquid feeling in her stomach, as she watched her own flesh and skin appear from under the hare's fur.

Then she realised she was on her hands and knees, feeling the weight of clothes on her back. She stood up, shivering slightly. She tried to smile. "Your door worked like a witch's gate, Atacama. Thanks!"

"But why were you a hare at all?" asked Atacama. "Didn't you find Mr Crottel? Didn't he lift your curse? Was it a waste of time?"

"Not a waste at all," said Theo briskly. "It was extremely useful. We now know that the Keeper is still a baby and the curse-hatched are taking advantage of her infancy to grow stronger. So I must find the first toy, deliver it to the nanny, free the curse-casters from the feast and remove the curse-hatched from the Hall. Give me the riddle answer to get back in and I'll go on this quest myself."

Beth said, "But we have to—"

"And don't say that you have to come with me because of your promise to Molly and her need to escape her worsened curse." Theo smiled. "I've worked out how Molly can get round it without the rest of you putting yourselves in more danger."

"How?" asked Beth.

"Molly no longer changes when she crosses from one garden or farm to another, but she did change when she ran onto Mrs Sharpe's land, into Mr Crottel's garden and out of the Keeper's Hall. So I think her curse has undergone one simple but significant alteration."

"What alteration?" asked Molly.

"The trigger to change back has altered, so you no longer shift when you cross human boundaries, only when you cross magical boundaries. You won't change when you jump your aunt's garden wall, but you will change when you enter Beth's wood. Witches' gateways work, but so will many other boundaries."

Molly nodded. "So I won't be trapped as a hare, it'll just be harder to find a place to change back."

"Not that hard," said Theo. "I can create a magical boundary by drawing a line in the air. Even Innes can manage it with a bag of salt and a bit of concentration. So long as you're with someone who has a little magic power and a basic magical education, you can change back." He grinned at them all. "So even though I'd enjoy your company, you don't have to come on this quest in order to save Molly from a terrible fate."

Beth shook her head. "It's not that easy. Didn't you see how long it took her to change back when we came through the door? Molly, you must have noticed!"

Molly sighed. "It was only a bit slower than usual this morning, but just now it felt like I was stuck between hare and human for ages."

"If the shift gets slower and slower, then sometime, maybe next time, you won't change back to a girl at all." Beth touched Molly's hand gently. "I know you like being a hare, and I know you think I nag you about dark magic and curses. But you nearly didn't turn back at all. It's not worth the risk, not any more."

Molly looked away.

Beth sighed. "You keep saying you want to lift the curse. But I'm not sure you ever really mean it."

Molly said, "I'm sorry. I do mean it when I say it, but it's really difficult to hold on to the right decision. When you tell me becoming a hare is dark magic, and remind me of the risks of this worsened curse, and ask me to my face what I'm going to do, then I know I should lift the curse. And I have tried to lift it! But then the next time I shift and leap and run, it feels so natural, it's hard to remember why it's wrong. Sometimes shifting to my hare-self is useful. Sometimes it's fun. Sometimes it even saves us from danger. It's not easy to choose to lose that. So it's not as simple as you make it sound."

"Molly, it's a curse. It was cast by a man who hates you, to hurt and kill you. And if you don't lift it, it's going to damage you and perhaps destroy you. So look at me and tell me what you need to do."

Molly clenched her fists. She looked into Beth's leaf-green eyes. "You're right. It's a curse. I need to get rid of it. I need to confront Mr Crottel and force him to lift it."

Beth raised her eyebrows. "The whole curse?"

"Yes. Ok. Yes. The whole curse. I need to get rid of the whole curse. As soon as possible." Molly turned to Theo. "Thanks for offering to go on the quest alone, but Mrs

Sharpe said the curse-casters would be more likely to lift curses if they were grateful, so I need Mr Crottel to be grateful to *me*, not you. I need to come on this quest."

"Me too," said Beth. "I want to make sure Molly gets another chance to be rid of this dark curse."

"I made a promise to Molly," said Innes. "So let's find that toy, take it to that nice old lady, then get all those casters out of there."

Atacama nodded. "This time I'm coming with you. I can't sit here thinking you're dead again. Where will we find this rainbow toy?"

"She didn't tell us," said Theo. "We have to work that out ourselves."

Beth said, "While we're thinking, we have to stay out of sight. Once Corbie realises we aren't in the Hall, he might come back here with his crows to hunt for us and—"

"Corbie's hunting for you? Why?" asked Atacama.

Innes said, "He found the guards in heaps behind the door after Beth and Theo defeated them, and realised someone had got through without a token. They got a good look at us while they were chasing us round the Hall."

Atacama sighed. "The crows will ask my bosses why I let you in. I'll be in so much trouble." He lay down again, head on his paws. "I'd better resign this post and offer to take a new job with a new riddle."

"But if you're not on sentry duty, how will we get back in with the toy?" asked Innes. "You have to stay here."

"I can't. I'm a security risk, and I have to admit that to my bosses before Corbie tells them." He swiped his paw against a bell hidden by the door, then stood up. He looked even worse than he had when they came out. Ears down, eyes dull, tail drooping.

"This is all your fault, toad-boy," said Innes. "This is the end result of you cursing him. He's about to lose his job, his whole reason for being—"

"It's not my fault," said Theo. "It's the end result of you using the secret he told you. He'd entirely recovered from my curse. It's your betrayal of his friendship that has caused this."

The two of them stepped closer, staring at each other. Theo was taller, even with his bald head, and Innes was wider at the shoulders. Molly didn't know who would win a fight between them, and she hoped she wasn't about to find out.

She moved forward to push them apart, but Atacama got there first. "It's *my* fault. I should never have accepted your help to find a new riddle. If they ever let me work again, I'll be guarding the back door of a supermarket with a riddle about mobile phones. Or they might sack me. I might be thrown out, to wander the wilderness, alone, abandoned..."

"Stop whining." Caracorum trotted round the nearest pyramid, tail high and ears pricked. "Why did you summon me? Have you done something stupid again?"

"I must admit an error to the high sphinxes. Can you cover my shift?"

"Of course, if this rabble get out of my way."

As they walked away from the door, Atacama said, "After I've been... reprimanded, I'll join you to search for the first toy. Where will I find you?"

Beth said, "We need to hide somewhere the crows won't look, so we can't go to any of our families' houses."

"Mrs Sharpe's farm is empty," suggested Molly.

"Her house will have witch's wards round it to keep her secrets safe," said Innes.

"What about the farm we rebuilt as curse-lifting homework?" said Theo. "It's empty too."

Beth nodded. "We'll wait at Cut Rigg Farm for you, Atacama."

The sphinx moved away from them, low to the ground, ears and tail flat.

Innes called after him, "And remember, you'll never have to wander the wilderness alone. You'll always have a home with me..."

The sphinx flicked his tail and walked round the corner of the pyramid.

Innes said, "Molly and Beth, you can ride to the farm on my back. This fundamental elemental magician can teleport there or fly or something."

"Not at the moment," said Theo quietly.

"Of course not." Innes stepped closer to Theo, getting right up into his face. "Because you can't store any power. You've moaned about that often enough. Can't you steal some power from a pigeon and fly? Or change into a toad and ask Beth to carry you in her pocket? You looked better with warts than that scarred head anyway."

Theo took a step back, breaking the tension. "Why do you hate me, Innes? You liked me when I was a toad. You chatted to me. Perhaps when you were telling me your secrets and fears, you should have considered that I wouldn't always be a toad, but that's not my fault. And it's no reason to be so... aggressive with me now."

Innes looked away. "I don't have any secrets or fears, actually. So you must have misheard with your tiny toad ears. And I don't like you because I don't trust you and because you cursed Atacama and because you do your magic by draining other people's power. You think you're this all-powerful magician but really you're just a magical parasite, and I've never liked fleas or midgies. So if you want to sleep at Cut Rigg Farm tonight, you can walk there."

"That's not fair," said Molly. "You take Beth. I'll lend Theo a bike and cycle there with him." She turned to Theo. "It's my aunt's rickety old bike, but it'll get you there."

"Thank you, Molly." Theo bowed slightly.

Innes snorted. "Oh for earth's sake, don't be *charming* as well." And he changed into a horse.

Innes galloped off, with Beth on his back, then Molly and Theo walked through the piles of casks towards her aunt's cottage.

"Sorry about that," said Molly. "Innes isn't normally so aggressive." Then she remembered his tentacles dragging her underwater. "Though he can be dangerous if you get in his way. It's probably best not to annoy him."

"I'm not trying to annoy anyone. I'm trying to protect everyone, by fixing the magical helix."

"Why don't you ask your family to fix it? You can't store power, but presumably they can. Why are you doing this on your own?"

"Why don't you tell your aunt about the curse-hatched? Why don't you phone your mum and dad about turning into a hare? Why are you coping with this curse on your own?"

"Because... Oh. Ok. Because I don't want to admit what an idiot I've been. Because I want to deal with it on my own. Because I don't want to get anyone else into danger or trouble."

"Yes. Precisely. Someone ambushed me, shaved my hair, stole my power, then transformed me into a toad. It will be easier to admit those failures to my family once I can tell them about a success too."

Molly led Theo into the cottage and shouted, "Hi, Aunt Doreen!"

They walked into the kitchen, where her aunt was peeling tatties at the sink. Molly glanced round, but there was no salt on the floor and they'd moved the furniture back before they left. There were no signs that the kitchen had been a temporary magical prison.

Molly asked, "Can my friend Theo borrow your bike, please?"

Her aunt turned round and smiled. "Of course."

Theo said, "Thank you very much, Miss Drummond."

"And I won't be back tonight," said Molly. "We're off for a sleepover with Beth." Molly realised she had no idea how long their quest would take. "I might stay with Beth tomorrow night too. So if you don't see me, don't worry about me."

"Two nights at Beth's? Is her Aunt Jean happy with that?" Molly nodded.

"Is this polite young man sleeping over too?"

"Yes. So is Innes." Molly stared at her Aunt Doreen, daring her to say anything.

Her aunt frowned, then took a deep breath. "I suppose we all need to move with the times. So I'm sure that's fine. Just be sensible. Don't light any fires in the woods, or do anything else dangerous."

Molly gave her aunt a hug. "I'm sure we won't do anything dangerous at all."

Chapter Eleven

The sun was setting as Molly and Theo arrived at the farm, but light was glowing at the farmhouse windows.

"We built this house." Molly grinned, as she leant her bike by the door.

"The toad didn't," said Innes, standing in the doorway. "He built the toilet."

Molly pushed past him into the fire-lit room. "Atacama! You got here before us! Are you alright?"

"Yes. The big bosses hissed and spat at me for half an hour, but I got off quite lightly. I should have admitted earlier that you'd helped create my riddle and therefore knew the answer. But because you spoke the answer before I let you in, I got off on a technicality. Until I receive a new riddle, I'm off the rota, then I'll be on probation, with Caracorum as my supervisor. She'll love being my boss…"

Theo said, "But if you're not guarding the Keeper's door, we have no way back into the Hall."

Beth said, "We don't have anything to take through the door yet, so let's not worry about that now." She pointed at a linen bag. "We stopped off at my house for food. While we eat, let's work out how to find the first toy."

Innes pulled out bottles of water and paper bags filled with baking. They sat in front of the fire, and ate sandwiches and scones.

Atacama asked, "So what did the old lady tell you about the object we're searching for?"

"It's the first toy, a rainbow-maker," said Beth. "Nan told us it was made by the first snake."

"Does it have power of its own?" asked Atacama.

Beth shrugged. "It's just an antique toy. That wee one loves her toys. She has a huge room full of them."

"She wanted Molly as her new cuddly toy," laughed Innes. "Bunny!"

Molly shoved at his knee. "I'd better stay human next time I see the Keeper, so she doesn't dribble on my ears or wipe her nose on my fur."

Beth muttered, "You'd better stay human from now on, because you might never turn back."

Atacama said, "So, this is all you know: it's a toy, it makes rainbows and it belonged to the first snake."

They nodded.

"Have you heard of it, Atacama?" asked Beth.

"No. We have ancient mouse toys and old varieties of catnip at our ancestral home, but no rainbows or snakes."

Theo said, "I could research the first snake in our archives, but the curse-hatched are taking over so fast that

I don't have time to go home, search through thousands of scrolls, then come back."

Atacama said, "We'll have to think our way round it."

Theo nodded. "There are myths about a snake creating the world, or circling the world, or becoming a rainbow in the sky. So, a snake creating a rainbow-maker as the first toy is plausible. But an ancient toy from the very start of the world will probably still be treasured and guarded."

Molly sighed. "This won't be easy."

"If it was easy, Nan would have got it herself," said Innes.

"Did she only save you from the crows so you could go on this quest?" asked Atacama.

Beth shook her head. "It was Molly's idea, bringing a toy to distract the Keeper while we free the curse-casters. Nan's just a nice old lady who changes the Keeper's nappies and washes her teddy."

Innes passed round a bag of scones. "So, assuming the first snake has shed her skin for the last time and is no longer alive, who would have the rainbow-maker now?"

Molly lay on the hard-packed earth floor and looked at the wooden roof. "We could ask the wyrm."

"What?"

"The wyrm we freed from a curse the night we built this farmhouse. I know it was a sort of dragon, but it was also a sort of serpent. A snake. It might know stories about the first snake that none of you know. And it owes us a favour. Why don't we ask the wyrm?"

"Because we have no idea where it is," said Innes.

"It only left here a few days ago and it was huge. Can't we track it?"

"I could try," said Atacama. "My nose is more sensitive than a human nose."

"We won't need to smell the wyrm," said Beth. "We can just look for broken branches and crushed plants. With its full weight on the ground, it must have left a trail."

Innes nodded. "We'll need daylight to follow a trail. Let's start first thing in the morning."

They agreed a sentry rota, then took turns sleeping by the embers of the fire and standing at the doorway staring at the starry sky.

Molly was woken by Beth speaking far too loudly in her ear. "Wakey wakey! Rise and shine! First light, time to get going!"

Molly moaned. "It's still dark outside."

"There's a glow on the horizon. Time to get up."

"No need to be so happy about it," grunted Innes.

"Come on, everyone! We have a wyrm to hunt!"

After Beth bullied them cheerfully to their feet, they ate dried-out sandwiches for breakfast, then washed their faces and filled their bottles at the nearest burn.

They started to follow the wyrm's trail, a subtle line of squashed and bent vegetation leading from the farm towards the Cairngorms. Whenever they lost the visible trail, on rock or springy heather, Atacama sniffed delicately and led them forward until they saw another crushed plant.

They walked and they walked and they walked.

"We only freed this wrym last week," said Molly. "How far can it have travelled?"

"It could have gone all the way to the English border," said Innes. "But it has no reason to go that far. It'll have found food, then somewhere to sleep. It could be round the next hill."

Molly thought of the wyrm's huge jaws. "Do we want to wake a sleeping wyrm?"

"Will it recognise us?" asked Theo.

Innes laughed. "It won't recognise *you*, toad-boy, so you'd better keep back."

But it wasn't round the next hill they trudged up and over, or the three hills after that.

"This is hard work," said Beth.

"If it's work," said Molly, "can your kelpie work ethic help us, Innes? Can we walk faster, like we built faster and dug faster last week?"

"Some people do this for fun, so it doesn't count as work." He sighed. "Do we have any scones left?"

"No."

So they walked and walked and walked.

Then they walked higher, up steeper slopes. The air grew colder and clammier.

"We're almost into the foothills of the Cairngorms," said Innes. "I didn't think we'd have to come this far."

They climbed the next rounded hill, into cold grey mist. Molly shivered, wishing her fleece was thicker. "Can we still follow the trail in this?"

Beth nodded. "The wyrm has been heading southwest on a fairly straight course for the last few miles."

They climbed higher. The mist got thicker.

Molly shivered again and the skin on the back of her neck tingled. "I feel like someone's watching me," she murmured to Beth.

"Me too," said Beth. "Are we being followed?"

Innes turned round. "There's nothing behind us."

So they climbed higher, into the mist, following the wyrm's trail.

Molly heard a faint chuckle.

Beth said, "Stop. There's definitely something else here."

They gathered close together on a broad heathery hilltop. Despite the mist, they could see the ground all around them. And there was no one there. No one in front, no one behind. No one following them.

Molly said, "Are we just imagining this?"

Atacama, the hair standing up along on his spine, whispered, "I feel watched. I feel spied on."

Theo said, "Let's keep moving."

As they walked forward, the mist in front of them swirled and thickened and became a huge grey man, his mouth wide open as if he was laughing, empty blackness behind his grey teeth.

But his laughter was silent. And Molly heard a squeaky chuckle from their left.

They all stepped away from the misty giant towering above them.

"Back the way we came," said Innes.

As they turned, the mist swirled behind them, thinning in places, thickening in others. And a misty man blocked that way too.

Molly whirled round and saw two more giants, blocking more routes down the hill.

All their wide-open mouths were laughing silently, with great black voids behind their teeth. But Molly could hear soft chuckles from lower down.

"They're big, but they're not solid," said Innes. "You can see the hills behind them. They can't hurt us. We can just walk through them."

He walked confidently towards the grey giant blocking the wyrm's trail. He strode at the man's wide left leg. And he banged into it, fell back and sprawled on the ground.

The misty giant bent over and picked Innes up in his see-through fist. Innes dangled from the grey fingers, his arms and legs hanging down. The huge man raised the boy towards his open mouth.

Innes shifted. But the giant's fist stretched to keep hold of the white horse.

Then the fist began to tighten and squeeze.

Molly heard the horse scream, a high-pitched neigh of pain.

The misty man threw the horse to the ground, hard, like a ball he wanted to bounce. Innes smashed onto the heathery hill and lay still.

The giant raised his foot above the white horse and stamped down.

Chapter Twelve

Innes shifted back to a boy, rolled out of the way of the huge grey foot crashing down, and scrambled towards the others, clutching his ribcage.

"Ok. They can hurt us. So we need a different tactic."

The four misty giants stood still, thick arms hanging by their sides, cloudy white eyes staring at the group huddled on the hilltop.

Innes said, "They're big and strong, so they probably aren't fast. If we all sprint, even on human legs, we can run between them and escape. On three… One, two, *three*!"

As they ran towards the open misty spaces between the men, that mist swirled and gathered. And four more grey giants stood there, laughing soundlessly, creating a complete circle around the hilltop.

"Between their feet," yelled Innes.

Molly ran for the gap between the nearest giant's feet, her head not even reaching his knees. But his right foot moved swiftly and she felt a soggy thump in her side as the grey man kicked her back into the middle of the circle.

She landed with a thud and saw another misty man kick Atacama in the belly. The black cat soared through the air, yowling, to land in a messy heap beside her.

Innes, Beth and Theo were nearby, breathing hard or groaning. They'd all been kicked into the centre.

"They're fast too," said Atacama. "Do we attack? With hooves and claws and teeth?"

Innes said, "If they can double in number whenever they want, we can't defeat them with a simple attack. This is strong magic. This is toad-boy's area of expertise."

Theo shook his head. "Not today. I don't have enough power."

"They only attack us if we try to get away," said Molly. "Maybe they just want to keep us here. Should we find out why? Should we talk to them?"

Beth nodded and called out: "Greetings, men of the mist. We are merely travelling through these hills. We don't intend to stay long or do any damage. Please let us pass."

The men answered. All of them, opening their mouths and roaring silently.

But Molly only heard one voice. Not a booming voice from high up; a lighter voice from low down, over to her right.

The little voice said, "You may not pass over our hill without our permission."

"So we'll ask for your permission," said Beth. "We are a dryad, a kelpie, a sphinx, a magician and a human, on our way to ask advice from a wyrm. We mean you no harm. If you let us pass, we will be off your lovely hill in moments."

"No." There was a high-pitched giggle. "It's too late to ask permission. You've already trespassed."

Innes muttered, "But there's no law of trespass in Scotland—"

"Shhhh!" hissed Atacama.

Beth said, "We would happily return to the base of the hill, ask permission properly, then climb up again."

"No. You have offended us. You have crossed our hill without our permission. So you will stay on this hill forever. You will become part of the hill."

"Become part of the hill? How?" whispered Molly.

"Die and rot and become fertiliser for heather, I assume," said Innes.

"You will stay here forever. There's no point trying to get away," giggled the voice, as another ring of giants materialised out of the mist, forming a tall wall round the summit of the hill.

"Anyone got any ideas?" murmured Beth. "Anyone even know what they are?"

"They might be the Grey Men of Ben Macdui," said Atacama. "People who've encountered a Grey Man often mention a feeling of dread and the sensation of being followed. But I've never heard of so many at once, so far from the Cairngorm plateau, nor of them trapping people forever."

"You wouldn't hear about it," said Innes, "if the people they trap never get away."

"If I shift and run low, they might not notice me. Then I could fetch help," suggested Molly.

"No!" said Beth. "You'd risk being stuck as a hare for the rest of your life!"

"If I don't, then we'll all be stuck here for the rest of our lives. Quite short lives. It's worth the risk. I'll run back to Craigvenie and tell your families."

"It's not worth it," said Beth. "There's nothing our families can do that we can't do ourselves. Do these grey men have a weakness?"

Theo was sitting on the heather, staring at the first grey man. "The mist swirled as they were created, so they're probably formed from tiny water droplets, which should follow the basic laws of physics."

Molly muttered, "I'm not sure anything I've met in the last week has followed the basic laws of physics."

Theo frowned. "We could try heat to evaporate the water droplets or cold to freeze them."

Innes said, "Beth, can you make a fire here?"

"There's no wood, just this scrubby heather, which wouldn't burn high enough to affect creatures that size." Beth turned to Theo. "Can you make fire?"

He shrugged.

"Of course you can," said Molly. "You made flames dance round Innes's head, just to show off. And don't say there isn't enough power here, we're surrounded by hills."

"But to create enough heat to alter the state of that monstrous quantity of water, I'd need to channel so much raw power that I risk damaging myself. Normally I store power before I use it, so I can tame it and control it. Using elemental power in its raw form is very dangerous. I'd probably harm myself more than them."

"Coward," said Innes. "We all face a slow *boring* death, and you're worrying about yourself."

"Stop whispering and mumbling," said the voice. "We want to hear the wind on our hillside, not your moans."

"Stop talking or *what*?" yelled Innes. "What can you do that's worse than trapping us here to rot?"

"We could pull you apart. You can stay on our hill forever just as easily in bits as you can in your current shapes."

The grey men flexed their fingers and cracked their knuckles. Silently.

"No more talk," whispered Beth. "I'd rather die now attacking these things, than wait for them to pull us apart." She stood up.

Theo sighed. "There's no need for everyone to risk themselves until we see what I can manage." He laid the palms of his hands on the earth under the heather.

Then he stood up. He pressed his hands together and drew them slowly apart. A bright golden chain appeared between his palms, with flames flickering along its links. He pulled his hands wider apart. The chain grew longer, with more and more burning links.

Then his arms were at full stretch and the chain was drooping under the weight of its burning golden links.

He flicked his right hand and the chain fell away. He grasped it in his left hand and whirled it above his head. The chain grew even longer and the flames burnt taller.

Molly, Innes, Beth and Atacama ducked as the chain scalded the air above their heads.

Theo whirled the chain faster and longer and hotter. Then he threw it up into the air.

He kept his left hand circling and the chain whirled above them, creating a burning hoop in the air. The chain rose and the circle grew.

The small voice squealed, "What are you doing? Stop it! Sit down and die quietly!"

The loop of flaming chain rose higher than the grey men's heads and grew wider than the circle they stood in.

The grey men, roaring noiselessly and flapping their hands, stepped forward, foggy fingers reaching out for the group on the hilltop.

"Stop it!" the high-pitched voice screamed.

Theo lowered his hand.

The loop of chain dropped to the height of the grey men's shoulders and started to tighten round them. They shrieked silently and stepped forward again, bashing into each other.

"You're pulling them towards us," yelled Beth.

"Sorry, it's the only way..." Theo flicked his hands.

The red-gold flames turned orange, then yellow, then the fire-chain was burning white hot.

The grey men stumbled inwards, trying to get away from the heat.

Molly and Beth wrapped their arms around their heads and crouched down as the giants' huge feet crashed closer and closer.

Molly heard a hissing sound and looked up. Where the chain touched the grey men, the mist was burning off, steaming into cloudy wisps then vanishing. The giants' heads and bodies were fading away.

But their feet were still stomping, stamping and shaking the ground.

The voice was screaming, "NO, STOP, NO!"

Theo brought the chain lower and lower, burning hotter and hotter, until the giants' legs were steaming away too.

Molly rolled out of the way of a pair of massive panicking feet. She banged into Atacama, as the feet hissed and steamed then slowly vanished.

The chain fell to the ground with a thud, burning its way into the heather. A few final misty toes bounced about, then disappeared in a puff of steam.

The chain sank into the earth, leaving a fiery circle in the heather. Innes and Beth stamped out the flames.

The voice squealed, "You've scarred my beautiful hill!"

Molly saw a small grey knobbly man, running away downhill, wailing and hitting his own head. "That's what attacked us? A little gnome thing?"

Beth said, "We have to get away, before he finds more

weather to trap us with. Thanks for giving us this chance, Theo."

Innes nodded. "I admit the toad-boy did find their weakness. I might even shake his hand, but... where is he?"

They looked round the summit.

Theo had vanished.

Chapter Thirteen

Molly pointed to the ground. "Theo's here. But he doesn't have a hand for you to shake. He's a toad again."

They crowded round the warty sand-coloured toad, who was squatting in the centre of the smoking circle.

Beth sighed. "Poor thing. But we can't stay here." She lifted the toad up, shoved him in her pocket and led the way as they all ran down the slope, still following the wyrm's trail.

They didn't stop running for half a mile.

Beth gasped, "I think that's a safe distance. Should we continue the wyrm hunt or take a look at Theo?"

Molly said, "Theo first."

Beth put the toad on the ground and they all sat in front of him.

They stared at the toad. The toad stared at them.

"How do we change him back?" asked Molly.

"Do we have to?" asked Innes.

"Don't be horrible," snapped Beth.

"No, really," said Innes seriously. "I actually prefer him like this. It's quieter, isn't it? No one bossing us about or showing off. He's a restful sort of toad. I always liked him when he was a toad. Let's just, you know, leave him as he is. Not interfere with the natural way of things."

"He did this to save us from the grey men," said Beth. "We have to turn him back."

Molly said, "Talk to us, Theo. Tell us what you need."

Innes snorted. "He can't talk. That's one of the nicest things about him right now."

"He can communicate," said Molly. "We've done it before. A croak for yes, silence for no?"

The toad croaked once.

Molly asked, "Can you turn back by yourself?"

The toad stayed silent.

"Can we help you turn back?"

Silence.

"Would another stone egg help?"

Silence.

"What about a kiss?" said Innes. "So you can turn back into the charming prince we're all so fond of."

The toad crawled towards Innes, stared at him, then crawled away again.

Innes laughed. "Fair enough. Don't say I didn't offer."

Molly sighed. "Could we donate some life energy to you?"

"Stop offering him your life-force," said Innes. "There's lots of power in the hills around us. He just can't use it. Can you?"

More silence.

"You can't use the raw power," said Beth. "You need stored power."

The toad croaked.

"He stored power in his hair," said Beth. "And since we first saw him, his hair hasn't started growing back. Not even stubble."

"Gosh, is he going bald already?" said Innes. "At the age of what? Twelve? Thirteen? That's a bit embarrassing."

"It's not a joke," said Beth. "If his hair doesn't grow back after the attack, he might never regain his full powers."

"If someone else gave you a lock of hair," said Molly, "could you store power in that?"

The toad croaked, then shrugged.

"That's a maybe. It's worth trying." Molly looked round. Her own brown hair wasn't even shoulder-length, Innes's blond hair was cut close to his scalp and Atacama's black fur was smooth and short. But Beth...

"Beth, you have lots of lovely long purple hair."

"Yes, ok. Anyone got scissors?"

Molly shook her head and looked at Innes. "Could you use your fish teeth again?"

Innes pulled a small red penknife from his pocket. "I didn't want my pike jaws to be the team's portable sharp object again, so I brought this. It's my mum's old hoofpick, but it has a wee pair of scissors too."

He handed it to Molly and she eased the tiny scissors out. Then she lifted up Beth's mass of long fine hair.

"If I cut some from underneath, it won't show, much."

"Just get on with it."

Molly hacked off a length of soft purple hair. "We should plait it, so it stays together."

"This isn't just a way of storing power," said Atacama. "This is also a gift from us to Theo. I know we don't always like his attitude—"

"Or his curses," muttered Innes. "Or his ambushes. Or his icy cages. Or his voice. Or his face."

"But we're a team," said Atacama. "So we should weave hairs from each of us into the plait. Molly, can you pull a few hairs from my tail?"

Molly tugged gently at the tip of his tail, and pulled out half a dozen silky black hairs.

Then Beth chopped a lock of brown hair from behind Molly's right ear.

They all turned to look at Innes.

"Really? You think I want to give toad-boy *anything* of mine?"

Beth said, "If we want to keep working together, this has to be from all of us."

Innes sighed. "I suppose he can be quite useful. And it's probably no fun being stuck as a toad." He leant forward and Beth hacked pale hairs from the nape of his neck.

Molly held the top of the long lock of purple hair, while the dryad plaited. Beth twisted in short hairs from Atacama, Molly and finally Innes. Then Molly tied the plait loosely round the toad's saggy neck.

They all stared at the toad again. He stared back.

Nothing happened.

Innes said, "If toad-boy really can absorb power from the hills, he can do it while we're walking through them."

So Molly picked the toad up, and they trudged along the wyrm's trail, muttering about lunch (which no one had brought) and tea (which wasn't likely to be any more filling than lunch).

Every so often Molly put the toad on the ground. "If you're going to change, I'd rather not be carrying you when you do!"

But he didn't change. He just looked resigned and floppy. So, each time, she put him back in her pocket and kept on trudging.

"How far have we walked now?" she asked.

"Hundreds of miles," said Innes.

"No more than ten miles," said Beth. "It feels like more because of all the up and down."

"We don't have to go much further," said Atacama. "I can smell it now. Not the trail, but the wyrm itself. We're very close."

They stopped and looked round.

They could see sloping hillsides, tussocky grass, dry heather, grey stone. No scales or tails.

"Where does the trail lead?" asked Molly.

Beth pointed past some crushed grass. "Up there."

They looked up the slope to the low round hill ahead. But they couldn't see a wyrm.

On a green field last week, the wyrm's purple, russet, grey and gold scales had been bright and obvious, but on the hillside they would be perfect camouflage. The wyrm was the same colour as the heather, bracken and stones.

Molly half-closed her eyes. There was a strip of hill where those landscape colours were arranged in diamonds and lines, where she could almost glimpse the smoothness of scales against the roughness of the ground either side.

"I see it. It's coiled round the summit."

Molly walked a few steps up the slope. Now she could see spikes lying flat against the wyrm's spine and the ruff of skin gathered against its neck.

The wyrm was huge. And asleep.

Molly sighed. "We'll have to wake it up..."

She turned round. Her friends were behind her, looking nervous.

"It will remember us, won't it?" she asked.

"I'm sure it will," said Beth.

"But will it remember us before or after it's swallowed us?" murmured Innes. "I'll wake it, if you want."

"You yelled at it; I spoke to it politely. It's safer if I wake it." Molly took another step forward, then stopped. "If it's going to eat me deliberately, it seems a shame for it to eat Theo accidentally as well." She took the toad out of her pocket and put him on the ground.

The toad crawled away from the wyrm.

"Coward," said Innes.

The toad crawled further away and collapsed, all four legs splayed out. Molly saw the plait of hair round the toad's throat glow, then spark, then crumble. The toad squirmed and grew, sprouting toes and fingers. Suddenly Theo was sprawled on the heather.

He curled up, moaning. Beth ran over to him. "Are you ok?"

Theo took a deep breath, uncurled and stood up. "I'm fine. Thank you."

"Did you break the curse again, with the plait?" asked Molly.

"No, that wasn't the curse. All the raw power ripping through me to control the fire-chain weakened me. I think the toad form was waiting to ambush me when I couldn't resist. So it's not the curse, more an echo of the curse. But your gift allowed me to store enough power to change back. Thanks! And you've found the wyrm?"

Molly nodded. "I'm going to wake it up."

She climbed the slope and laid her hand cautiously on the huge scaly head. "Hello, Mr Wyrm. Sorry to disturb you, Mr Wyrm."

The wyrm's eyes opened, its head rose and its ruff flicked out.

Molly took a step back. "Hello, Mr Wyrm. I hope you remember us. We freed you from the curse at Cut Rigg. We'd like to ask a favour."

The wyrm tipped its head to one side.

"Do you understand me?"

The wyrm yawned.

Molly tried to keep her voice steady as she looked at the wyrm's spear-length fangs. "We're searching for an ancient rainbow-maker toy, created by the first snake. Have you heard of it?"

The wyrm flicked its tail. Atacama leapt into the air sideways, to avoid being knocked over.

Molly looked at her friends. "Even if it can understand me, how can it answer me?"

Theo said, "Let me try."

"The wyrm won't recognise you as one of the curse-lifting team." Molly turned to the wyrm. "This boy was the toad who built the outhouse."

"He built the toilet," muttered Innes.

As Molly stepped back, Theo sat cross-legged in front of the wyrm.

Then he spoke. Not in English, nor in a sibilant snaky language. He spoke in a language with high clicks, deep burrs and a rhythm that matched no language Molly had ever heard. Even so, she felt she almost understood.

After Theo introduced himself, the wyrm answered, in a hissier voice, but with the same clicks and rhythm. Molly almost grasped that too. Were they chatting about the weather?

Then Theo spoke more firmly, with rising inflections. Asking questions. Asking favours.

The wyrm answered.

Molly whispered, "I think the wyrm knows where the rainbow-maker is."

Innes said, "Yes, I almost understood that."

"I never thought I would hear this," said Atacama. "It's like something out of the old myths."

Theo bowed his head and the wyrm bowed back.

Theo stood up and walked to the others. "The wyrm owes us gratitude and a favour. She thinks the circling snake, the oldest serpent she knows, may have played with the rainbow-maker in his youth. She'll help us find him."

"What language were you speaking?" asked Molly.

"I was speaking the first language, the language all our ancestors spoke before they built the tower of Babel, in your Biblical times. I'm not fluent, but it can be useful."

"Where is the circling snake?" asked Atacama.

"On the coast."

"The coast!" said Beth. "But we've just walked towards the heart of Scotland, directly away from the sea."

"I can go on my own," said Innes, "or carrying a couple of you."

"We're all bound to this quest now," said Theo. "Anyway, the wyrm can only speak to me and she's most attached to Molly."

"Even though I called her Mr Wyrm..." murmured Molly.

Beth said, "So we must all go."

"How?" asked Innes. "I can't carry all of you."

Theo spoke to the wyrm again.

She nodded.

Theo smiled. "The wyrm will carry us north on her back. I hope everyone has good balance and no one gets travel-sick, because this could be a bumpy ride..."

Chapter Fourteen

"I can gallop as fast as this wyrm can slither," said Innes. "I'll follow and pick up anyone who falls off. Atacama, will you run with me?"

Atacama shook his head. "I would be honoured to travel with this noble wyrm."

Innes smiled. "Probably wise. Cats are built for quick hunts, not endurance running."

Molly and Beth looked at each other, then at the wyrm's wide spiky back.

"It might be a rollercoaster ride," said Molly, "but I'll give it a go."

"Me too," said Beth.

But it wasn't anything like a rollercoaster ride, because the wyrm didn't move up and down, she moved from side to side.

The serpentine movement might look smooth and elegant to any witnesses on the summits of the surrounding hills. But for the passengers on the wyrm's back, with hands clutching onto spines or claws hooked over scales, it was an extremely disorientating way to travel: constantly jerking from left to right as well as forward, at breathtaking speed.

Molly felt dizzy if she looked down at the ground under the wyrm, so she tried to keep her eyes on the horizon, even though that meant Beth, Atacama and Theo were whipping in and out of view in front of her.

Eventually she got used to the wyrm's rhythm and learnt to move her shoulders to compensate, so her head wasn't jerked about. She started to enjoy the scaly sprint through the landscape and she was almost sorry when they arrived at the coast.

Molly could see a fishing village to her left, but the wyrm avoided it, just like she had avoided all the towns on the way.

Then the wyrm paused at the top of a cliff and nosed through the gorse on the cliff edge. She found a narrow gully, at a slightly shallower angle than the steep rockface, and slid down to the beach below.

"That last bit was too much like a rollercoaster," Molly gasped, as she clambered down. Theo, Beth and Atacama joined her on the sand.

The wyrm twisted her head and looked along her own curved body, then bit off one of her own spines. She spat the spine at the sand in front of Molly's feet.

The wyrm spoke to Theo, they both glanced at the sun, then she moved towards the calm sea.

"She's not had a bath since she was trapped under the

farm," explained Theo. "She'll return at sundown, in less than an hour."

They watched as she slipped into the sea and vanished from sight.

"Can wyrms swim?" asked Molly.

"They're related to Chinese river dragons," said Atacama. "They love water."

"Isn't the wyrm going to introduce us to the circling snake?" asked Beth.

"She promised to bring us here," said Theo, "but was reluctant to speak to the snake herself."

Molly prodded the spine with her toe. "Why did she spit this at me?"

"The spine is the key."

"The key to what?" Molly picked it up. "Where is the snake?"

Theo pointed to the cliff. "In that cave."

Molly looked round. The yellowish sandstone was tiger-striped with darker lines of rusty rock. There was an arch at one side of the cliff-ringed bay, near the rockfall gully they'd slid down, and lots of small holes along the base of the cliff, with one big dark entrance at the other end of the bay.

And there was a white horse on the clifftop.

Beth waved the kelpie over to the narrow gully. Innes shifted into his boy form and scrambled down the rockfall to join them.

"That wyrm is fast! I almost lost you. So, what are we looking for?"

"A big snake in a dark hole." Molly pointed at the cave entrance.

"Where's our serpentine guide?"

"Gone for a swim," said Beth. "We're on our own."

They walked together towards the cave and peered inside. All Molly could see were dark rock walls leading towards a black space.

Theo said, "I can't make light, in case I become an amphibian again."

"I can make torches." Beth headed towards the sea.

While Beth walked along the tideline looking for driftwood, the others waited at the cave's mouth.

"I sense strong magic in there," said Theo. "Caves are often full of interesting energy, because they have the earth all around rather than just underfoot. But there's something else here. Something ancient and powerful."

Beth returned with two driftwood branches. She murmured to them and they started to burn with blue-tinged flames.

"A salty light." She smiled. "The life of the tree and the life of the sea. Good things to take with us into the earth."

Beth handed Molly a torch and the light brightened the cave mouth, which was more colourful than Molly expected. The walls were striped with red, orange and yellow ridges, and a low green band where the tide rose each day. But the darkness of the cave stretched further than the warmth of the light.

"What does the circling snake circle?" asked Molly.

"That fishing village?" suggested Beth.

"The North Sea?" wondered Atacama.

"The whole planet?" asked Theo.

"Let's find out." Innes took the first step into the cave.

The cave was just wide enough to let them walk side by side, and its pebbly floor sloped slightly downwards. Molly stumbled over an empty beer can. "Would an ancient snake really live in a cave that locals use for parties?"

After fifty paces, the cave bent to the left, so Molly could no longer see sunlight when she glanced back. After a hundred paces, they reached a rock wall. There was nothing at the back of the cave but a tideline of litter.

"You sensed something ancient and powerful, did you?" Innes kicked a bottle towards Theo's feet. "You're such a fraud."

"Whatever is in this cave can't be obvious or all the locals would find it."

"The wyrm gave us a key." Molly held up the long grey spine. "Where's the lock?"

They examined the wall at the back of the cave, holding the torches close. There were lots of cracks in the rock, creating a pattern like squint tartan.

Atacama pointed a paw at the very centre of the rock wall.

Molly saw a tiny round hole where several cracks met. She passed her torch to Theo and gently pushed the spine in. And in, and in, and in. Until the arm-long spine was almost completely hidden.

Nothing happened.

She pulled her sleeve over her hand, folded it to make a protective pad, jabbed her palm at the jagged end of the spine and shoved it hard. It disappeared completely into the stone.

The wall creaked, cracked along one diagonal line, split and separated. Beyond it, they could see another rocky tunnel.

They moved forward cautiously. This tunnel was carved from darker rock than the cave. They walked on, the blue-ish torchlight flickering.

Soon the tunnel opened up into a much wider space.

"Is it here?" Innes whispered.

"Shhh," said Atacama.

They kept walking forward.

"How will we see it with so little light?"

A voice hissed, "Ssssee it? You don't need to see it, because *I* can see *you*."

Beth held her torch high.

They were in a huge cave with cliff-like walls and a rocky ridge at the back.

As Beth and Theo waved the torches, they realised the cliff to their right wasn't a cliff. It was a massive snake's head. And the ridge in the floor where the head was resting wasn't rock, it was a tail. They'd found the head and tail of the circling snake.

The snake was black. Black scales, black eyes, black tongue flicking between black fangs. But behind the surface of the black scales, the torches seemed to be lighting up stars and galaxies at impossible distances.

"Ssssmall ones, come closer."

The snake's head and mouth didn't move as he spoke. The words were inside Molly's head, hissing like a badly tuned radio. They all took a few paces forward.

"Ssssomeone I trust must have given you a key. Who let you in?"

They looked at each other. Who wanted to talk to this gigantic creature?

Atacama shrugged, then spoke. "We freed the Wyrm of Cut Rigg from a curse. She gave us the key so we could ask you a favour."

"Sssso ask your favour, little kitten."

"We seek the first toy, created by the first snake. The rainbow-maker."

"Ssssomeone has come to ask for my precious toy, at last. Why now?"

Theo said, "We wish to present it to the Promise Keeper, who's currently a baby and being influenced by those who want curses to last forever. This gift will help us restore balance."

"Ccccertainly an ambitious aim. But why you? Who are you?"

Beth said, "We are simply a group of friends trying to lift a curse."

"Ssssimply? Nothing is simple. Each of you state who you are, what you are and why you personally need my rainbow-maker."

So they each spoke in turn.

"I am Molly, a human, cursed to be a hare at inconvenient times. I need the rainbow-maker to lift my curse and to free a witch called Mrs Sharpe from the Keeper's Hall."

"I am Beth, a dryad. I promised to help Molly lift her curse, because she lifted mine. I need the rainbow-maker so I can keep my promise."

"I am Atacama, a sphinx. I also need the rainbow-maker to keep my vow to Molly."

"I am Theo, an elemental magician. I need the rainbow-maker to restore balance to the curse arc of the helix."

"I am Innes, a kelpie. I need the rainbow-maker, because I promised to help Molly—"

"Ssssspeak the truth, kelpie." The snake's voice rattled louder in their heads. "Speak the truth to me."

Innes looked over at Beth, then at Atacama and Molly.

"Ssssspeak the truth, or you all leave empty-handed!"

Innes looked up at the huge black serpent. "I need the rainbow-maker to rescue the curse-casters from the Keeper's Hall, because I'm scared the crows will come for me next, drag me to the Hall and keep me prisoner there. That's the truth, that's why I need your toy."

"Ssssneaky child. That is true, but it's not the whole truth. Tell me why you're scared, colt. Tell me why they would come for you."

Innes sighed. "Because I'm a curse-caster too. Because, last week, I cast a curse."

Chapter Fifteen

"Ssssuch a fascinating announcement, young kelpie. Do tell us more."

"I am a curse-caster." Innes's voice rang round the cave. "Did everyone hear that? I'm a curse-caster. I cursed someone who thoroughly needed cursing, but in doing so I let one of those vicious crows hatch from a stone egg. Now the crows are capturing casters to protect their young and... and I'm afraid they might come for me next."

"Innes, what have you done?" whispered Beth "Who have you cursed?"

"Shhh," said Atacama. "Not here. Not now."

The snake laughed inside their heads. "Sssso your friends are not happy with your honesty! But I enjoyed it. I'm too old to play with toys; I prefer to play with my visitors. You have amused me, particularly your faces as this pretty little pony spoke the truth. So I will give you my rainbow-maker, because you have entertained me and because what happens next might entertain me too. But I will also give you a warning: restoring balance is not easy; sometimes the helix twists the other way. Are you prepared to risk adding the complication of an ancient and powerful artefact to your problem?"

"Yes," said Theo.

The snake laughed again, then the tip of his black galaxy-dotted tail pointed at the cave wall to their left.

They looked over. On a small shelf of dark rock, Molly saw a glint of light.

"Ssssnakes shed possessions like skins, but I have kept this all my life. You may take it."

Molly was nearest, so she walked across the cave towards the shelf. As she got closer, she saw a long fang-shaped crystal, bending even the faint light in the cave into all the colours of the spectrum, creating pale rainbows on the wall behind.

She picked the crystal up, holding its icy smoothness carefully in the palm of her hand.

"Ssssad to see it go," hissed the snake. "But eager to watch, from here and from everywhere I am, to see what will happen when you take that relic of my hatchling-hood out into the world. Farewell, little ones."

"Thank you," said Beth.

"We're grateful, noble snake," said Atacama.

Theo said, "It's been an honour—"

"Sssstop now. I am weary of you. Take the trinket and go." The snake closed his eyelids, slowly, like black moons eclipsing dark suns.

They walked out of the snake's cave, through the tunnel

and into the smaller cave. The rock-wall door slid shut as soon as Innes, walking half a pace behind the rest, stepped through.

Beth dropped her torch on the floor, slammed both hands into Innes's chest and pushed him up against the cave wall. "You cast a curse? After all we've been through, you cursed someone? How could you?"

Innes didn't push back. He just stood there and let her shove at him. But he answered quietly, "It's complicated."

"It's not complicated!" Beth yelled. "It's simple. Curses are dark and evil, and you don't use them. It's simple."

Molly heard laughter hissing in her head. "Atacama's right about not arguing in the cave. Let's get out."

Beth pushed at Innes again, slamming him harder into the wall. Then she picked up her torch, apologised to the wood for dropping it and walked away.

They followed her to the mouth of the cave, no one meeting Innes's eyes.

When they reached the beach, the sun was just above the horizon and Molly could see a V-shaped ripple out at sea. Perhaps the wyrm was already on her way back.

Beth handed her torch to Molly, then stood right in front of Innes and shouted, "You told the snake the truth, but you've been lying to us. We're meant to be your friends. So stop lying and tell us what you've done."

"I wasn't lying to you. I just didn't tell you about... something. About one thing."

"One thing? One curse? One life ruined? You're on a

quest trying to lift a curse, and you've *cast* a curse. That's not just a lie, that's a betrayal!"

Molly put her hand on Beth's shoulder. "Don't yell at him, yet. We don't know what he's done or why. Innes, tell us the whole story."

"You know most of it already…"

Molly heard splashes above the gentle rhythm of the waves. "The wyrm's on her way back. Maybe we should leave this until later." She glanced over her shoulder.

And saw a line of dark-red creatures lumbering out of the sea.

"What are they?"

Everyone looked round.

"Because they don't look friendly."

The creatures had large human-shaped heads, but very wide mouths and one glowing yellow eye each. They had human shoulders and torsos, and arms so long they were dragging their huge clenched fists on the sand. Their lower bodies were almost horse-shaped, with four legs, but each leg had a flapping fin down its length and ended on a flipper-like foot.

They were already forming a semicircle from the shoreline to the cliff, standing at a distance but trapping Molly and her friends at the cave mouth, blocking their way to the gully, blocking their exit from the beach.

Innes said quietly, "They're not friendly. They're nuckelavee, from the north. They're carnivorous, but they don't usually hunt in packs."

The largest nuckelavee opened its mouth, showing jaw-wide blades of bone rather than individual teeth. It spoke in a booming voice: "Give us the rainbow-maker and we'll let you go. Refuse and we'll eat you, then take the rainbow-maker anyway."

Innes called across the sand, "Allow us to discuss your generous offer." He turned to the group. "That's clear enough."

"What, we give them the rainbow-maker or we die?" said Molly.

"No, we give them the rainbow-maker or we fight." He glanced over at the nuckelavee. "There are fifteen of them. That's an uncomfortably large number. But we have to try. I'll use hooves. Beth and Molly, use your torches. Atacama, use your claws. Toad-boy, you'd better sit this out, in case you become a toad again."

"I don't need to sit it out, I just need to pace myself. I can probably deal with six or seven, if the rest of you can manage two each."

"That sounds fair," said Innes.

"Wait a minute. This is impossible," said Beth. "I don't *want* to give them the rainbow-maker, but there are three times as many of them as there are of us, and they have blade-teeth and huge arms—"

"They also have one weakness," said Innes. "They can only come out of the sea onto the land once a day. If we push them back into the water, they'll have to stay there. Get them in the water, stay out of the water ourselves and we can win."

Theo nodded. "I'll take the ones furthest from the sea, because I can throw them in from a distance."

Innes raised his voice. "We're coming to give you the snake's toy now."

"Another lie," murmured Beth, taking her torch back from Molly.

Innes sighed. "Give it a rest, Beth. In a fight, truth and lies can be weapons. If they think we're giving them what they want, we can get nearer to the water before we attack. So this lie lets us choose the battleground. Molly, show them the rainbow-maker."

Molly held the crystal up, seeing it properly for the first time. It was twice as long as one of her fingers, wide and smooth at its base, and sharp at its tip. As she held it up, the base faced the low sun and a sudden rush of light from the tip blinded her. She blinked, then angled it so that the light wasn't shining straight through.

The five of them walked slowly towards the nuckelavee.

As they got closer, Molly realised why the nuckelavee looked dark red. It wasn't the colour of their skin, because they didn't have any skin. It was the colour of their muscles. She could see thin lines of black blood pulsing through veins, and thin lines of yellow tendons stretching at knobbly white joints.

"Stop there!" shouted the largest nuckelavee. "Send the holder of the rainbow-maker forward alone."

They all stopped.

"Should I go?" Molly said, nervously.

"No," whispered Innes. "Not on your own. Everyone, remember, push them into the sea, don't let them push us up the beach."

Suddenly, Innes shifted into his horse form, knocking Molly one step sideways as his body took up more space.

Molly shoved the crystal fang into her pocket and zipped it up.

Beth spoke a word and the torches in the girls' hands flamed higher.

Atacama's fur rose on his back and he began to growl.

Theo kicked off his sandals and pressed his bare toes into the sand.

Then they all ran at the skinless one-eyed sea monsters in front of them.

Molly saw a silver shape appear in the air above Theo. A curved hook, dangling from a rope that faded into nothingness before it reached the height of the cliff behind them.

The hook swished through the air, caught the largest nuckelavee under the armpit, lifted the monster off the sand and swung it over the sea. The hook vanished and the monster fell into the water.

The other nuckelavee didn't react immediately, so Innes kicked one hard in the chest, three times, knocking it back until it toppled into the sea. Atacama attacked another with teeth and claws, and forced it a handful of steps back into the water.

Molly and Beth jabbed their torches at the nuckelavee

nearest them. The monster Molly was attacking took a step back. But only one step. All four flippery feet were still firmly on the sand.

Theo had created another hook to lift another nuckelavee. The horse and the cat were attacking two more monsters, but the leader was shouting from the sea, "Get away from the water's edge!"

Now the nuckelavee were lumbering further from the sea.

And they were fighting back. They were swinging their heavy fists, on arms longer than Molly's arm and torch combined.

The monsters didn't move fast on their finned and flippered legs. They didn't have to, because they could swing those huge pendulum arms with terrifying pace and momentum.

Molly still hadn't forced any creatures into the sea. But she was keeping one at bay with her torch. By thrusting the flames at the nuckelavee's skinless chest and single eye, she'd pushed it two more steps towards the gently fizzing surf.

Suddenly another nuckelavee, behind her, started flinging its fists at her.

She ducked down.

The nuckelavee she'd been attacking took a step forward. She stood up and jabbed at its face again. It screamed hoarsely and stepped back.

Then a fist slammed into her shoulder from behind and she stumbled forward. Another fist hit her in the ribcage and she fell to the side.

Molly whirled round with the flames, trying to drive both nuckelavee away from her. She jabbed at the one nearest the sea again, yelling, "Get back!"

"Move up the beach," yelled their leader. "The one in the cloak is the most dangerous. Knock him down first, then mop up the rest."

Molly thrust her torch at the nuckelavee near the sea, but it didn't move. It just lifted both arms and brought both fists hurtling down towards her head.

She fell to the ground and rolled out of the way. She banged against the flippered legs of the other nuckelavee and slashed her burning torch against its bare flesh. It roared and stepped out of the way.

Another fist swung down and crunched against her thigh. Her leg went numb and she knew she wouldn't be able to put weight on it yet. She held tightly to the torch and kept stabbing upwards with the fiery end.

She could see another nuckelavee dangling from a pale silver hook, so Theo was continuing to use his magic. But there were still a larger number of nuckelavee on the sand than in the water. Molly's thigh started to hurt, the numbness fading, so she tried to stand up.

Suddenly she was rising through the air, even though she hadn't found her feet yet.

She was being lifted off the sand by the large damp fingers of a nuckelavee, one hand clamped round her left ankle, one hand clamped round her left shoulder. She waved her torch around, but the other nuckelavee grabbed her right arm and twisted. She dropped the torch.

Molly was lifted towards the first nuckelavee's mouth.

She jerked and wriggled, but the nuckelavee tightened its fists.

She twisted round to look at the wide-open mouth: dark and stinking, with two long sharp guillotine-like blades embedded in the fleshy gums.

"Don't eat her whole," a voice yelled from the sea. "She has the rainbow-maker. Just bite a bit off!"

"Which bit will I bite?"

"The hands," said the other monster beside her. "The hands that waved the fire."

Molly bunched her fists and struggled to hide both hands behind her back.

"Or the head. They can't do much once you remove their heads. And the skulls are nice and crunchy."

Molly screamed as the nuckelavee adjusted its grip and brought her face closer to its skinless jaws.

She swung her right fist up and whacked the nuckelavee in its single eye. It yelled, a gust of salty breath blowing over her face.

She punched again and jerked her whole body violently at the same time.

The nuckelavee loosened its grip.

And her shoulder slid out of its fingers. Now she was dangling by one leg from its other huge hand.

She couldn't punch its face again, but as she hung upside down, she could stretch her arm to reach her dropped torch. It was burning feebly on the damp sand, spluttering and dying. Which was just as well, because Molly couldn't reach the handle of the torch, she could only reach the burning end.

Molly lunged at the torch, grabbed the glowing end, gasped at the pain in her fingers, swept it off the sand, threw it up and caught the cool end as it fell.

She waved the torch gently in the air, to get oxygen to the fire and encourage it to burn brightly again.

Then she raised the torch and burnt her own leg. She aimed the flame at her own ankle, where the nuckelavee was gripping her tight.

It howled and dropped her.

She leapt to her feet and whipped the torch hard at the nuckelavee's injured eye. She ignored the fists pummelling her back and struck again and again, until the nuckelavee lifted its hands to protect its face and toppled into the sea.

Molly turned to see the other nuckelavee swinging its fists at her.

She didn't have the energy to do all that again, so she backed away.

Glancing over her bruised shoulder, she saw Theo leaning against Beth, with Atacama and Innes using their fast feet to keep three attacking nuckelavee off him.

Molly ran towards them, aware that she was bringing another attacker to the party, but unable to defend herself much longer. She saw rips in Theo's cloak, blood running down his face and a small silver hook dangling at an unconvincing angle beside him.

"Stop now, Theo," said Beth. "Let us do the rest."

His head dropped down and the hook vanished.

Molly stabbed her torch at a nuckelavee's hand as it swung towards Theo's neck.

The nuckelavee jerked back, then laughed. "Your fire won't last for ever."

Molly knew it was right. The flames were smaller, the wood was shorter, and her burnt hand and leg were stinging.

Theo whispered, "I can't hook any more of them, but they don't know that. If they still think I'm the main threat, perhaps I can get them into the sea another way..."

He pulled himself up, waved his hand to create a pale shadow of a hook above his head and shouted, "Come and get me."

Then Theo walked between Innes's hooves and Atacama's claws, and staggered down the beach. Right into the sea.

The nearest nuckelavee stepped after him, following him into the waves.

"NO!" yelled their leader. "No! You idiot!"

But another nuckelavee had already reached out to try to grab Theo, and stumbled into the sea.

Which left only two monsters on the beach, looking confused, being yelled at by the nuckelavee in the water, being kicked and slashed and burnt in a sudden burst of energy from the kelpie and sphinx and torch-bearers on the beach.

In a flurry of hooves, claws and sparks, they drove the remaining nuckelavee into the sea.

Now, all fifteen of their attackers were trapped in the salt water.

But so was Theo.

Chapter Sixteen

Theo stood, bruised and thin-faced, in the water. Fifteen meat-coloured nuckelavee gathered round him.

Molly saw their arm muscles tense and dark blood rush through their veins, as they crashed their fists together.

The leader said, "Don't eat him yet, he could be useful." Then it turned to the group on the beach. "Now we have a hostage. Give us the snake's fang and we'll give you the boy. Otherwise we'll each take a bite out of him, and let the fish have what's left. "

Innes, who'd changed back to his human form as soon as all the nuckelavee were in the water, answered, "Do what you want with him. We don't like him anyway."

"I'm not bluffing," said the nuckelavee. "We will devour him, unless you give me the rainbow-maker."

Innes folded his arms. "I'm not bluffing either. That boy is dangerous, irritating and a threat to my position. I'll happily watch you eat him."

Beth said, "But Innes, you can't—"

"If you're feeling squeamish, you flimsy little dryad, close your eyes or turn your back."

"Innes, I won't—"

Molly grabbed Beth's elbow and whispered, "Shut up! If you stop and think for even a second, you know Innes doesn't mean it. You know he has a plan. Stop distracting him."

Innes nodded at the nuckelavee. "Go on. What are you waiting for?"

The leader scowled. "This is your last chance. Give me the rainbow-maker and I'll spare the boy."

"But I want the rainbow-maker and I don't want the boy."

The nuckelavee shrugged, its muscles squirming on its shoulders. "This will disappoint our employer, who was very keen to get that fang. But the boy does look tasty, so who's hungry?"

Fourteen nuckelavee raised their knobbly fists.

Theo, who was standing straight with his hands flat on the surface of the gently moving water, murmured, "No. Wait. Please."

He lifted one of his wet hands and splashed sea water on his face. Then he sighed. "Oh Innes, how can you be so cruel? After all we've meant to each other? After all that teamwork, all those kind words, all those oaths of lifelong friendship? How can you treat me this way?"

His voice was soft and trembling. His eyes were wide and pleading. And both his hands were flat on the surface of the sea again.

Innes laughed. "Oh Theo, you know I never liked you and your fancy magic tricks, and you know I'm never going to swap this old toy for your life."

At a signal from their leader, the nuckelavee reached towards Theo.

Molly unzipped her pocket, wondering if she'd mis-judged Innes, wondering if she could save Theo herself.

Then she saw Theo grin.

She glanced at Innes.

He was grinning back. "We're not going to save you, Theo. You'll have to do it yourself."

"Myself? Like this, you mean?"

Theo lifted both hands and slapped them down on the surface of the water.

The water shivered. Then the water slid back. Like the sea had breathed in suddenly, the water surged backwards, leaving a wide strip of seabed free of water. Including the seabed under Theo's feet and the nuckelavee's flippers.

The nuckelavee screamed and collapsed to the damp sand, oozing pink slime from their skinless flesh.

"What happens if they come out of the sea twice in one day?" asked Molly.

Innes shrugged. "They dry out rather fast."

Theo stepped over the groaning bodies and walked up the beach.

Innes said, "Did I blether long enough for you to have a refreshing dip in the sea? Have you got more energy now?"

Theo nodded. "How did you know what I needed?"

"I didn't think you were stupid enough to walk in there unless you had a way out. But I thought a bit of misdirection, and a few extra minutes in the water before you did your elemental thing, might help."

"So did you not mean it, when you said you wanted to watch Theo get eaten?" Beth asked as they walked away from the distant sea.

"Of course not. He's annoying, but he's handy in a fight. How many did you fling into the sea with your skyhook, Theo?"

"Six. Slightly fewer than I'd hoped. How did you do with your hooves?"

"Three. Not including the couple we sent in as a team when you had your wee moment of drama at the end."

"Three's a pretty good score."

"Thanks, Theo."

"Thanks to you too, Innes."

They reached the rubble at the bottom of the cliff and sat down to watch the moaning nuckelavee drag themselves towards the far-off edge of the sea, leaving glistening trails of slime behind them.

Beth said, "Is everyone ok? Any injuries?"

Molly looked at her singed jeans. "Bumps, bruises and burns, but nothing serious."

"Me too. Though of course my wood didn't burn me. Sorry, I should have asked it not to burn you either."

"I've broken a claw," said Atacama. "But otherwise I'm fine."

Innes shrugged. "I'm ok."

Theo slid down the rocks to lie on the sand.

"Are you alright?" asked Beth.

"I'm not a toad, I'm not being eaten by sea monsters and we still have the rainbow-maker. So, yes, I'm fine."

Molly patted her pocket. "Who's their 'employer'? Who sent them here to steal the toy?"

"Were they waiting for us specifically?" wondered Beth. "Or for anybody who left that cave with the rainbow-maker?"

But before anyone could answer, Molly saw the wyrm heading up the sand, slaloming elegantly around the retreating nuckelavee.

Theo pulled himself up and limped forward to greet the wyrm.

He spoke briefly to her, then turned back to the group by the cliff. "She's offered to take us to any location we choose in Speyside. Where should we go?"

"Somewhere we can rest and eat, before completing our quest," said Atacama.

"Not somewhere the crows might be watching," said Beth.

"Go back to Cut Rigg," said Innes. "I'll buy food in one of the towns we bypassed, and meet you there. Anyone got money?" Molly gave him her one pound coin and Beth found a fiver in the sequin-covered purse in her back pocket.

Innes clambered up the gully and shifted to a horse

at the top. He reared on the cliff edge, the pink light of the sunset shining on his white neck and flanks, then galloped off.

Theo laughed, but Beth said, "He's not getting out of that difficult conversation about curse-casting, however much he shows off."

The wyrm halted in a perfect circle around the farm buildings, exactly where she'd been trapped for years.

Molly, Beth and Theo slid off. Atacama leapt down. The wyrm spoke briefly to Theo, and nodded to Molly, who nodded back. Then the wyrm sped off into the night.

"She doesn't like being reminded of her imprisonment," said Theo. "Perhaps we should have chosen a more diplomatic destination. Anyway, her debt to us is paid."

Beth lit a fire in the farmhouse fireplace, then they settled down to wait for Innes to bring their supper and an explanation.

Beth sat in a corner, a torch spinning between her hands. They all watched the flame carve a constantly vanishing circle in the air.

"I can't believe Innes has cursed someone." She sighed. "We've been friends since we were babies. I thought I knew him."

"You do know him," said Atacama. "He's ruthless, decisive and very protective of his rivers and his family.

You know that. If he's cursed someone, perhaps he had good reason."

"But how did he manage to curse someone?" asked Molly. "He's not a witch."

"You don't have to be a witch to cast a curse," said Beth. "Lots of the curse-casters in the Hall – the fairies, the mermaid, the giant – won't have been magically trained."

"Can anyone cast a curse?" Molly asked.

"Not anyone," said Beth. "You need magic to make a curse stick. So only those who were born with magical abilities, or those who have learnt magic, can cast curses that work."

Molly frowned. "So everyone here except me could cast a curse."

"Yes," said Beth. "But we wouldn't want to. It's not a nice thing to do."

"Actually, Molly, you could cast a curse," said Theo. "The magic which transforms you into a hare is embedded in your bones, and you can already manipulate that magic by shifting when you want. You're more powerful than you think."

"But I've no idea how to use that power," said Molly. She noticed Beth's disapproving face. "And I wouldn't want to use it. That would be wrong, obviously."

They heard hoofbeats outside, then footsteps.

Innes walked in, holding up a bag. "Bread, cheese, fruit. Can we please eat before Beth tortures the truth out of me?"

So they ate in uncomfortable silence, with Beth and Innes sitting in opposite corners.

The money they'd found in their pockets hadn't bought much food, so the silent meal didn't last long. When there was nothing left except spirals of orange peel and crumbs on the floor, Innes said, "Ok. Can I tell you what happened, without lots of shouting and shoving?"

Beth nodded. "I'll listen to what you have to say."

Innes spoke slowly. "I didn't plan to do it. And I regret it, because I feel guilty about it and I'm scared of what will happen to me now I'm a curse-caster. But I also don't regret it, because I couldn't see any alternative.

"I don't think all curse-casters are evil, Beth. You've just shared a meal with Theo and you've been on Mrs Sharpe's workshop, so you obviously don't think they're evil."

"Theo is an ally on a quest, Mrs Sharpe is a teacher," said Beth. "You're my *friend*. I expect more of you."

"Sorry to disappoint you."

"Stop pussyfooting around," said Atacama. "Tell us who you cursed."

Innes looked down. He used his index finger to tidy the scattered breadcrumbs nearest him, piling them up neatly.

Then he said, "I cursed my dad. I cursed my own father."

Chapter Seventeen

Molly could hear rain outside and everyone's jittery breathing inside. No one spoke a word. Theo was staring at the wall, not wanting to get involved in a disagreement between friends. Atacama was doing his best impression of a statue, staring straight ahead. Beth was staring at Innes, open-mouthed. And Innes had his eyes closed, like he could block out what he'd just said.

Molly knew there was one vital question, and it didn't look like anyone else was going to ask it.

"Why?" she whispered. "Why did you curse your own dad?"

Innes opened his eyes and looked straight at her. "I'll tell you the whole story. It won't make sense any other way.

"Last week, when I told him we'd lifted the curse, Dad was delighted. He suggested the two of us take a trip up one of our tributaries, dive off our favourite high rock and swim together, to celebrate. We hadn't spoken properly since he ate those fairies and got our whole family cursed. But he was so relieved, he became really chatty. We were sitting on the rock, drying off after a race – which I won, by the way – and he told me that he only regretted eating those fairies *because he'd been caught*, and that over the years he'd got away with eating lots of other magical beings.

"I reminded him of the rule that kelpies don't eat magical beings or humans near our home rivers. He just laughed and said that by hunting on moonless nights or eating all witnesses, a kelpie can kill anywhere.

"At first, I thought he was joking, but then he boasted about eating a handful of solitary fairies and at least three brownies. And remember the fuss when that hiker went missing? That was my dad too.

"I asked him to stop. I asked him to promise that he wouldn't eat any more of our neighbours. But he said that kelpies are hunters and predators, and that dragons and tigers don't follow rules, so why should we?

"I know I'm a hunter. And I'm sure that when I'm older I'll go on a hunting trip to find challenging prey by other shores. But I won't hunt here, I won't hunt my friends and neighbours. It's not right and it's not sensible either, because it leaves the kelpie's family and the kelpie's river system open to revenge attacks. Like the fairy's curse that killed my big brother.

"Then Dad said he'd take me hunting by the Spey, one dark night soon. He wants me to be like him. Greedy, a rule-breaker, a danger to everyone around me... And I don't want that.

"I asked him again to promise never to hunt near our rivers. But he refused to promise, and he laughed at me for following the rules. So I cursed him.

"I didn't plan to, but because we'd been studying curses, that popped into my head as the most obvious way to stop my dad.

"I cursed him to turn to stone.

"He realised what I was doing and shifted to his stallion form to attack me. But I spoke so fast that he turned to stone as he reared up. The stallion statue toppled off the rock, into the deep pool.

"And that is why I cursed my father."

He glanced over at Beth. She looked away.

Molly watched Innes as he stared at the floor again. His fists, his jaw, his shoulders were clenched and tense. He looked ready to defend himself, to leap up and lash out, as soon as anyone criticised him.

What could she say? She couldn't say he'd done the right thing, but she couldn't say he'd done the wrong thing either. Perhaps she should just keep him talking until someone else thought of something useful to say. Molly remembered the questions they'd answered on Mrs Sharpe's workshop.

"Does the curse have limits? Can your dad lift it?"

Innes's face relaxed. "Yes, of course! I want him to lift it! The curse states that he will return to his human form every five days, for five minutes, and if he promises during that time to stop hunting in the Spey valley, the curse will be lifted. But if he ever again eats anything that can speak words or do magic, within twenty miles of the Spey or its tributaries, he will turn to stone forever." Innes almost smiled. "It was quite an effective curse, for one I made up on the spot..."

"Does someone have to be there to hear him promise?" Molly asked.

"I don't think so. That's what the Promise Keeper does, isn't it? Lift curses when the victim fulfils the conditions?"

Innes glanced at Theo, who nodded.

"But I'll go up there tomorrow anyway," said Innes, "and try to persuade him to promise."

"Does your mum know what you did?" asked Molly.

"No! Of course not! She thinks he's gone off on one of his long hunting trips. That's what I sort of suggested when I came back without him. She won't worry for a while. I suppose I'll have to tell her, eventually. But *how* do I tell her?" He flicked the crumbs around the floor, making more mess than he'd tidied up.

"So..." He looked round at everyone's shocked faces. "So I'm going to be in massive trouble with my mum. I can't even think about what my dad will do to me when he's free of the curse. And the curse-hatched might imprison me at that endless snooze-feast. There *are* consequences to what I've done. I'm not getting off with this scot-free. So perhaps you lot could just be my friends and help me through this, rather than staring at me like I'm a monster."

He paused. "Though my dad is a monster. And I turned him to stone. So maybe I'm a monster too. I just hope I can control it better than he can."

Innes looked round them all again, clearly more nervous than he'd been facing a row of nuckelavee.

Molly couldn't think of any more questions, and she didn't know how to answer his plea for support.

But Beth had an answer. "You used dark magic. That is unforgivable."

"I prefer to think of it as grey magic, Beth. I used a curse to stop my dad eating other magic users and to prevent our family being cursed in revenge. I was defending myself, my family, my rivers, you and your family, and all our neighbours. How can that be a bad thing?"

"Surely you could have done something else to stop him? Surely a curse wasn't your only choice?"

"Yes. True. I could have killed him. Do you think that would have been a better solution? I don't. This way, he has a choice: he can change his ways, he can become a good neighbour and father again."

"Whatever he becomes," said Beth, "you will always be a curse-caster, and I can't forgive you for that."

Innes's shoulders slumped.

Beth frowned. "There's only one way I might be able to forgive you. Lift the curse *now*. No conditions, no limits, just lift the curse."

"You want me to set him free?" asked Innes. "Without a

promise? Without a guarantee that he won't murder more magic users and human beings on our riverbanks?"

"There must be other ways to stop him. You have uncles, aunts, other senior kelpies in other rivers. Ask them to help. Ask them to enforce your rules. You don't have to make yourself a monster too."

"You really think I'm a monster? Because of one curse?"

Beth bit her lip and nodded.

"Is he a monster?" Innes pointed at Theo. "He cursed Atacama. And I bet that wasn't his first time. I bet he uses curses whenever they suit his big fancy magical questing purposes. I bet he always has a good reason and always makes the curses as small and gentle as possible, so no one calls him a monster, but I bet he's cast curses before."

Theo smiled. "You know me better than I thought, Innes."

Beth looked at Theo. "You cast curses *regularly*?"

Theo shrugged. "Curses are just magical tools. But I give you my word that no one is currently suffering under a curse cast by me. Innes is right. I use light curses and I design them to be lifted fast. And my victims usually forgive me, like Atacama has forgiven me. Haven't you?"

"Not quite," growled the sphinx. "Not forgiven exactly."

Innes grinned. "See. It's almost an epidemic. Everyone's doing it."

"Not me," said Beth. "Not ever. And I'm not trusting

this quest to dark-magic users. I never really trusted you, Theo, we were always on different quests in the same direction. But Innes, you're my friend. I did trust you. You must lift that curse before we take the rainbow-maker to the Hall."

"No. I can't release him without the promise. He's dangerous – to me now as well."

Beth stood up. "You must do it now. You've no idea what that curse is doing to you."

"It's making my friends treat me like a toad – sorry Theo – and it's making me nervous about crows, but on the whole that curse is doing more good than harm."

"It's not that simple," said Beth. "When I enter the trees' world, I see what they see. And they see dark-magic users growing rotten inside. It's like… it's like a pear, which looks lovely and sweet and fresh on the outside, but when you slice it open, it's brown at the core."

"Fruit metaphors," groaned Innes. "Dryads *always* use fruit metaphors."

"That's a fruit simile, actually," said Beth. "But the only way to stop the rot eating away at your core is to remove the curse completely. It's the same with Molly. Perhaps shapeshifting isn't doing her physical damage, but manipulating and enjoying the dark magic of a curse can't be doing her any good, inside."

Molly frowned and put her hands over her stomach. When she controlled her curse, deliberately shifting to a hare to race Innes or escape the curse-hatched or protect her friends, was that damaging her? Was it turning her into a dark-magic user, as well as a hare?

Beth continued, "That's why Molly has to get Mr Crottel to lift her curse. And you have to lift that curse on your dad. Promise me you will."

Innes stood up too. "No. I can't. I don't think the curse is eating me up inside. There's more than one kind of magic in this world, Beth, and your gentle flowery nature magic is not the only good or useful kind."

Beth shook her head. "If you won't lift the curse, you can't come back to the Hall with us. How can we know you won't curse us all? If you think a curse is an appropriate solution to a problem, none of us are safe."

"You don't really think I'd curse a friend—"

"You cursed your own father!" she yelled.

"Yeah, my father the murderer."

"But Innes, just because he did something wrong, doesn't mean you did something right when you stopped him. Embracing dark magic leaves its mark."

"I've not embraced it. I just used it once."

"Now you've done it once, it will be easier to do again. You might curse me or Molly or Atacama or Theo, or your mum, or your teachers, or anyone else who annoys you. Can you guarantee you won't curse anyone else?"

"I don't know!" he yelled. "It depends how much you nag me!"

Beth backed away from him, holding her burning torch between them. "That is exactly why I can't work with you, and exactly why I can't be your friend any more."

Molly stood up. "Calm down, both of you. Once we've taken this ancient toy to the Keeper's Hall, Beth, you can take Innes off your Christmas list. But let's stop arguing now and finish the quest."

Beth said, "I can't work with him while he has the taint of a curse round his core. He can't be part of our team."

"I can't, but Theo can?"

They all looked over at the slim scarred boy sitting quietly in the corner.

"Theo is not actually part of our team," said Beth. "Theo is on another quest entirely. But you can't come with us, Innes. If you won't release your father from the curse, then Molly must release you from your vow."

"What?" said Molly.

"He's only part of our team because he promised to lift your curse. If you release him, he won't have to come with us." She looked at Molly. "Release him from his vow."

"Can I do that?"

"You have to. If you release him, he can act like the selfish self-centred predator he really is and go off on his own again."

Innes laughed. "The selfish predator who just hunted a herd of cheese rolls for your tea?"

Beth didn't look at him. "Molly? Release him. Send him away."

"Is that the only reason you're all here? Because you made a promise? I thought you were helping because we were friends." Molly sighed. "I don't want help from anyone who doesn't genuinely want to help me.

"So, I release Innes from his promise, but I also release Atacama and Beth. I can take the rainbow-maker to the Keeper's Hall on my own. I can free Mr Crottel, Mrs Sharpe and everyone else, on my own. If Mr Crottel won't lift my curse out of gratitude, then I'll challenge him in the archaic way. On my own. No one has to help me if they don't want to. So you're all released from your promise."

Innes stared at her for a moment, then walked to the doorway.

Beth took Molly's hand. "I'll help you lift your curse, not for the promise, but for our friendship."

Atacama said sadly, "I can't justify bending my own sphinx's vow any further, without the vow we made together to balance against it. So I'd better return home. I'm sorry."

Theo spoke for the first time since Innes and Beth started arguing. "I didn't make a vow. But I'm going to the Keeper's Hall anyway, so I'm happy to help you lift your curse, Molly."

Innes was still standing in the doorway. "I suppose I should stay away from the Hall, in case the crows try to keep me there. So I should leave you to your quest."

Innes walked into the darkness. Atacama followed him.

Beth said, "Thank you, Molly. We can still do this, the two of us." She glanced at Theo. "The three of us, following the same path to different ends."

Molly listened for hoofbeats leaving. She only heard the rain.

Theo stood up. "What should we—?"

A figure walked out of the darkness into the firelight.

"I hear there are two girls trying to lift a worsening curse, and a magician with the balance of the world on his shoulders. If anyone wants a helping hand, or a helping hoof, I'm happy to re-join the team."

Molly held out her hand. "Welcome back, Innes!"

Theo nodded at him and smiled.

Beth said, "You're here to help Molly and Theo? But you won't promise me that you'll lift your dad's curse?"

"I won't promise what I can't do. But I will promise that I won't leave him cursed for longer than necessary. I just hope that won't be forever."

Beth sighed. "Ok. I can't stop you helping. But this doesn't mean that I trust you or that I like who you're becoming."

"I only stepped round the corner before I turned and came back." Innes grinned. "Just for dramatic effect. Maybe Atacama's trying to upstage me. I wonder how long he'll take to come back…"

They looked at the doorway. They waited. But the sphinx didn't return.

Chapter Eighteen

"Atacama is bound by a different vow," said Molly. "That's fine. We can do this ourselves."

She sat by the fire and the other three joined her.

Molly said, "So we have to get into the Hall, through a door guarded by a sphinx. We have to give the rainbow-maker," she patted her pocket, "to the baby. Then Nan will help us find the door so we can get the curse-casters out."

"We have to get the curse-hatched out too," said Theo. "I have to remove their unbalancing influence on the infant Promise Keeper, then block the crowgate and negotiate with the sphinxes not to let the crows back through the door."

Molly checked her watch. It was almost eleven o'clock at night. "It's very late. Should we go now, or sleep and go in the morning?"

Innes said, "I don't think I could sleep."

"Me neither," said Theo.

Beth said, "I just want to finish this quest."

"Me too," said Molly.

They went out into the drizzle and Innes said, "We have two rickety bikes and one fit horse. Who wants to pedal and who wants to ride like royalty?"

"Beth and I will cycle, so you can take Theo," said Molly. "He's still tired after using all that raw power, and we might need him at full strength in the Keeper's Hall."

Theo and Innes looked at each other.

"Are you sure?" said Theo.

"Of course," said Innes. "I can't criticise you, now everyone knows my dirty secret. Come on, we'll meet the girls at the pyramids."

As Molly and Beth wheeled the bikes towards the road, Innes shifted. Theo climbed onto his back and they galloped off, Theo's pale cloak flapping over the horse's white flanks.

"You won't solve it," sneered Caracorum.

"Just ask your riddle," said Innes.

The golden sphinx faced Molly, Innes, Beth and Theo, between the high stone wall and the sweet-smelling pyramids, and asked:

I am the seedling to your tree, the ugly duckling to your swan.
I am the rock to your statue, the first chapter to your book.
I am the morning of the ancestor's riddle.
I am crying out for an answer.
What am I?

Innes frowned.

Beth shook her head.

Theo shrugged. "My brain doesn't do that. It sounds like gobbledegook."

Molly said, "Could we hear it again, please?"

Caracorum repeated the riddle. But it didn't make any more sense.

Molly sighed. "Can we have a chat before we answer?"

"Of course. You won't work it out."

They moved away and Molly said, "Anyone got any clever ideas?"

"An ugly duckling is a cygnet," said Innes. "Is that the answer?"

"Don't be daft!" snapped Beth. "A cygnet isn't a tree or a rock, it's a bird. We need an answer to the whole riddle, not a little bit of it."

"I'm just trying to help."

"It could be a leaf," said Beth. "Seedlings have leaves and there are leaves in books—"

"There aren't leaves in books!" Innes laughed. "Not unless you're pressing flowers."

"It's an old name for pages. That's why you leaf through a book."

"But you don't leaf through a duck or a statue. So 'leaf' doesn't make any sense."

"Is it the beginning of something?" said Molly. "The first chapter is the beginning of the story."

"What's the ancestor's riddle?" asked Beth. "Whose ancestor?"

"Caracorum was looking at Molly when she recited the riddle," said Innes.

"It's not about your nasty witchy ancestor, is it?" said Beth. "Did she have a riddle?"

Molly shrugged.

"Two riddles…" Theo sighed. "Caracorum's riddle and an ancestor's riddle. That's not fair. One riddle is hard enough!"

"But that's the riddle Caracorum asks everyone," said Innes. "So it can't be about Molly's ancestor. Maybe it's about her own ancestor?"

"About Caracorum's ancestor? About an older sphinx? Maybe the original sphinx?" Molly smiled. "So 'The morning of the—'"

"Of course!" said Innes. "Morning, duckling, seedling, crying! Is the answer 'ing'?"

"Don't be an idiot," said Beth, "'ing' is a sound, not a thing."

"Stop squashing each other's ideas," said Molly. "I might have the answer. A baby. The first chapter of a book and the rock before a statue are beginnings, and she was looking at me, because a baby is the beginning of a human. A cygnet is a baby swan, a seedling is a baby tree. And there's the baby from the riddle asked by the original sphinx. So could it be a baby?"

Beth said, "Of course. Well done."

Innes frowned. "I'm not... Oh, hold on! Crying out for an answer, that's because babies cry. So yes, it is."

Molly stepped forward. "The answer to your riddle is: a baby."

Caracorum bowed. "Correct. I can let your party of four through."

"Party of five, sister." Atacama strolled round the corner of the pyramid, his rain-speckled black fur glinting in the moonlight. "I let my friends find the answer themselves, in case you accused them of cheating if I helped, but now they've answered correctly, I'll be joining them."

"But sphinxes never go through the door!"

"Perhaps we should. Perhaps we should know what we guard. So, a party of five, going through, thank you, sentry."

Caracorum snarled. "This is a mistake."

"Probably," said Atacama. "But I let them go without me last time and that was an even worse mistake."

The golden sphinx nodded and stood aside.

They placed their hands and paws on the door and pushed it open. They walked out of the dark of the night, into the dark of the corridor. The door closed behind them.

"Do you think there are new guards?" whispered Molly.

There was a dusty silence, then a tiny CLICK.

"Yes, there are new guards," said a rattly voice. "Newly made guards who still ache and itch after being ripped apart the last time you vandals came through that door."

The torches flickered into life and Molly saw lines of warriors blocking the corridor. They looked scruffier and a bit squint, like they'd stepped off a collage in a classroom rather than a mosaic in an ancient temple. Some were cross-eyed, some had one arm longer than the other, some had mismatched armour and helmets. But they all had long sharp weapons.

The tallest mosaic man, with only one eyebrow but an impressive scowl, yelled, "Attack!"

"Wait!" shouted Molly. "You can't attack us. We have the token."

"We do?" murmured Beth.

"We have the object Nan asked for. That's a token, isn't it?" Molly unzipped her pocket and tried to pull the rainbow-maker out.

"She's bluffing," lisped a guard with gappy teeth.

"No, it's here, it's just a bit big to..." She twisted the long fang and eased it out past the zip, but everything else in her pocket tumbled out too: bus tickets, five pence, pocket fluff and pocket rubbish.

"Here." She held up the rainbow-maker.

"That's not the token."

"It's the toy Nan asked us to bring for the Promise Keeper. Surely this proves we have a right to come in."

The mosaic man shook his clinking head. "You can't just turn up with any old object—"

"Ancient object," corrected Theo. "It's not just old, it's ancient."

"You can't just turn up with any *random* object," snarled the guard, "and claim it's on Lady Nan's shopping list.

There's only one acceptable token and you've not shown it to me. Weapons ready, men."

"But... hold on..." Molly couldn't think of anything else to say.

"She hasn't shown it to you, but she does have it," said a short guard at the end of the line. He was probably made out of leftover tiles, because his skin was spotty and his sword was stripy.

"She has the token." He pointed at the floor. "It was in her pocket."

Everyone looked down. At a bus ticket, a five-pence piece, an old hanky, some orange fluff and a black feather...

The black feather from Mrs Sharpe's shop. The black feather of a curse-hatched crow.

Molly picked up the feather. "Of course. This is the token. This proves we have a right to come in."

"You may enter, honoured guests," said the leader of the mosaic men.

As Molly scooped the rest of her rubbish back into her pocket, the guards lined up against the wall.

Molly walked past the sharp swords and long spears, holding the black feather up like a shield. She whispered to Beth, "I had this feather last time too. Oops. We didn't need to fight them."

The door at the end of the corridor swung open into one of the rooms they'd sprinted through last time. It was the room filled with mirrors, vases, jewelled chains, a long table, and high windows showing a daytime sky.

Molly asked, "What is this room for?"

"This is the Chamber of Promises," said Theo. "The heart of the Promise Keeper's Hall, where all the promises are stored. The mirrors are curses, promises designed to do harm; those vases are enchantments, promises designed to do good; the chains up there are vows, promises which bind."

Molly said, "Is that why I saw myself in a mirror last time? Beside a pile of dog dirt?"

Theo nodded. "When it's placed anywhere on this table, the surface of the mirror displays the casting of the relevant curse. I'll show you..."

"I thought you hadn't been here before," said Innes.

"Several previous Promise Keepers left memoirs in the library at Alexandria, so the workings of the Hall are public knowledge."

"Only if you read the scrolls before that ancient Egyptian library burnt down a couple of thousand years ago," said Atacama.

"Or if your family saved most of them and you have to read every single one for homework," muttered Theo.

"So tell us how it works," said Atacama.

"Do we need to know?" asked Innes. "Shouldn't we just go and hand over the rainbow-maker?"

"This won't take long. I'd like to see if the records are correct. The earliest curses are on mirrors so old, they aren't even glass. But this," Theo picked up an angular mirror from the nearest rack, "this is less than a hundred years old, judging by the art deco frame."

He placed it on the table. "The casting of the curse."

They all peered over, and saw a woman shouting faintly in French at a girl. The girl's beaded dancing shoes started to glow with heat and the girl screamed.

The mirror misted over and the sequence started again.

Theo lifted it off the table. The image vanished and the faint yelling stopped. He carried the mirror to the head of the table, where there were two hollows in the smooth white surface.

"I think the left-hand hollow is where any attempt to lift the curse will be displayed. If the attempt is successful the mirror shatters. If the attempt is less successful, if it's not clear whether the conditions are met, the mirror cracks. When a mirror cracks rather than breaks, the Promise Keeper studies it and decides if the curse has been lifted or not. In the last few years, that judgement has almost always been in favour of the curse-caster, not the victim. This Promise Keeper never uses her discretion to be merciful."

"Because she's only a baby?" suggested Molly.

Theo shrugged. "Perhaps she sees things too simply, in absolute black and white rather than subtle gradations of grey. Or perhaps she takes biased advice from people who give her rice-cakes. Who knows?"

He laid the mirror in the hollow.

They saw the same girl holding a branch covered in small flowers, waving it at the woman. She was yelling at the woman, in a slightly panicked way, and the woman was laughing. The girl yelled the same word three times and the woman started to grow feathers on her arms, but the woman flicked her hands and the feathers sprouted along the girl's eyebrows and eyelashes instead. The girl shouted something else. The woman's throat started to grow scales, but she flicked her hands and the scales erupted on the girl's cheeks instead. The girl burst into tears and ran off, limping.

"A failed attempt at magical combat, which is why the mirror is still intact." Theo lifted the mirror up. "Magical combat is extremely risky. She challenged the witch and lost, so she ended up with feathers on her eyelids and scales on her face, as well as burning shoes.

"And the right-hand hollow should show the curse happening, with images from each time it's triggered." He placed the mirror in the other hollow.

They saw a different girl put different shoes on. The shoes glowed and the girl kicked them off.

"The Promise Keeper is also responsible for ensuring that every time the curse is triggered, there's enough magical power to make it happen. So when the Keeper touches a mirror, she puts a fraction of her own elemental power into the curse."

Molly watched a succession of girls and boys, all with similar faces but wearing increasingly modern clothes, put on a succession of party shoes. They all flinched with pain and kicked the shoes off.

Theo smiled. "It works, just like the old records describe. By watching every mirror here, you could study the history of curses through the ages, from every different culture and style of magic. Fascinating!"

"You can do your creepy homework later," said Innes. "Let's find the Keeper. I don't want to spend longer here than I have to."

He led the way to the main door and the white corridor.

Molly asked. "Can anyone remember which direction the baby's room was in?"

Innes and Beth both pointed left.

They heard a baby wail to their right.

Molly shrugged and turned right, towards a big carved door. They pushed the door open cautiously and saw a huge room with a high ceiling held up by two rows of pillars. At the other end of the room were a large throne, a fire flickering on a high black slab, and two figures standing by the fire.

Beth whispered, "Should we go in?"

The baby wailed again, her cries echoing round the red-and-gold striped pillars.

Molly touched the crystal fang in her pocket. "We came to give the toy to the baby. And she's here, so let's go in."

"Careful," said Innes. "I think that's Corbie near the fire. Use the pillars as cover."

They crept up the long dim room, moving from one wide pillar to the next. When they got close enough to smell the fire's spicy fragrance, Atacama and Innes were hiding behind one pillar, and Beth, Theo and Molly were behind another, slightly further back.

Molly peered round. She saw Corbie, in his ragged black coat, fetching logs from a pile of firewood; Nan, in her blue dress and white apron, adding wood to the fire; the baby, pale and shining, lying on a golden cushion on the floor.

Molly realised that the Keeper didn't look like a human baby. She looked like a moving statue, a perfect child carved out of white stone, decorated with gold and jewels.

Nan picked the baby up, and the baby wailed. "Not fire, not fire. Bath time now. Not fire."

The baby was bigger in Nan's arms than she'd been earlier; she was already almost a toddler.

Nan held the baby up. "Shush, my poppet. Ducks in the bath soon..."

She stepped nearer the fire.

"Duckies," said the baby. "Duckies splash."

The Keeper's gold curls and pearl teeth reflected the flames. The firelight created a halo of brilliance around her shining body.

The baby giggled. "Hot!"

Nan kissed her forehead. "I know, darling. It's very hot."

And she put the baby in the fire.

Nan stretched out her arms and put the giggling baby right into the centre of the flames.

The baby wailed.

The flames rose higher.

And the baby started to burn.

They all stared at the baby in the fire.

For as long as it took one flame to flicker and rise and lick at the baby's gold curls, they all stood still and stared.

Then they all moved.

Molly took a fast step forward.

But Theo grabbed her arm and swung her round, keeping her hidden behind the pillar.

Molly jerked her arm, trying to get free, trying to rescue the baby. But Theo's grip was strong, and he had Beth's wrist in his other hand.

He whispered, "Don't interfere. It's not what it seems…"

As Molly dragged her hand downwards, trying to break his grip, she heard Innes yelling in pain.

She twisted and looked round the pillar.

Innes was standing by the fire.

Innes had both hands in the flames.

Innes was grabbing at the burning baby.

Chapter Nineteen

As Innes tried to pull the baby out of the fire, Nan and Corbie ran round the slab and crashed into him, knocking him down.

Suddenly Innes was on the floor, hands under his armpits, hissing and gritting his teeth with pain. And the baby was still in the fire.

But the baby was smiling, laughing, waving at Innes on the floor.

Theo whispered, "See. The baby's fine."

Molly glanced at the other pillar. Atacama was crouched low behind it, tail flicking uncertainly.

Molly wrenched her wrist out of Theo's fingers. But as she watched the burning baby smiling and Innes rolling on the ground, she didn't think running out from behind the pillar would help anyone.

So she stayed hidden as Corbie grabbed Innes's collar, pulled him up and slammed him against the black slab, the kelpie's shoulders and back close to the flames.

And Nan reached into the fire to lift the baby out.

Molly could just see the baby in Nan's arms, gazing up at Nan's face, making pouting shapes with her lips. The baby was tiny, half the size she'd been when she was put in the fire, and she looked like a newborn rather than a toddler. She was still shining like mother of pearl and coils of gold foil.

"The baby's not burnt?" gasped Innes. "I thought—"

Nan interrupted. "Where are the others? Where are your friends?"

Innes scowled. "Friends! Some friends they turned out to be. They wouldn't have anything to do with me once they realised I'd cast a curse."

"You cast a curse? I can't keep track of them all. Did he cast a functioning curse, Corbie?"

"He cast a splendid curse on his father, hatching out a fine strong bird. We'd like to keep him and his curse safe."

Nan smiled. "You cursed your own father! How wonderfully classical! And you don't know where your friends are now?"

"No idea. I came back here myself, because I was afraid of what my family would do to me. I hoped you might protect me."

Nan nodded. "The curse-hatched are running a generous curse-caster protection scheme just now. You'll be safe here. But first, where is the rainbow-maker?"

"I don't know. After we collected it from a gigantic snake, that hippy dryad refused to work with me because apparently I'm tainted with dark magic. Then they were ambushed by nuckelavee, so I left them to it. I haven't seen the snake's toy since."

"Just as I planned. The nuckelavee will send me the rainbow-maker and we won't be bothered by those idealistic young curse-lifters again. But why did you interfere just now? Why did you barge into our ceremony?"

"Well… You were burning a baby. I wanted to save the baby from the fire. It's what most people would do, isn't it?"

Nan laughed. "How sentimental. So your friends are wrong, you're not entirely overcome by dark magic yet. But my lovely little baby didn't need saved. This is her night-time routine. Supper, fire, bath, bed."

"That's a little… unusual."

"The flames burn off the day. They burn off her growth and what she's learnt during the day. And I get a sweet little newborn again. If my darling Promise Keeper never grows up, she'll always need her Nan." She stroked the baby's cheek.

"We should lock this kelpie up," said Corbie. "He destroyed my flight feathers last week."

Nan looked at Innes. "Do we need to lock you up?"

Innes shrugged. "I don't want to leave. Everyone back home hates me because I cast a curse. I'm safer at your feast." He looked at Corbie. "I attacked you because of a vow that I've now been released from, so I've no reason to attack you again."

Innes blew on his hands. "I'd be grateful for some cold water. Then I'll leave you to your bedtime routine."

He tickled the baby's tummy. "If you visit me at the feast tomorrow, wee one, we can play peekaboo!"

Nan turned to Corbie. "Ask your guards to escort this young kelpie to the feast and fetch him ice-water."

Corbie snapped his fingers and three crows flew down from the shadows above the throne. Two of them changed into black-clad men, who grabbed Innes's elbows and led him from the huge room, as the third crow flew behind.

Innes didn't look back. He hadn't glanced over at the pillars once while Nan had been questioning him.

Molly held her breath. Did Nan and Corbie know they were there? Had Innes covered up for them convincingly enough?

The silver-haired woman and the sharp-faced man just kept chatting.

"Curse-casters are coming to us for protection now!" laughed Nan. "That's new."

Corbie said, "I don't trust him."

"What harm can he do? One bite of the feast and he'll become as sluggish as the other guests. Especially if he eats an actual slug. Do you think he'll swallow a slimy slug, my sweetie?" She lifted the baby above her head. The Keeper wriggled happily. "Just as well that interfering kelpie didn't pull you out of the fire too soon. You have to stay in long enough to burn off the whole day, don't you little one? We have to keep you young and immature, to keep your Nan in charge."

She settled the baby in her arms again. "This nightly fire keeps me in control, Corbie, but I'm still condemned by my curse to stand beside the throne. Never on the throne, always to the side."

Nan gestured at the flames. The fire collapsed into a black pile of ashes. "After thousands of years wiping the noses and bottoms, and washing the sweaty socks and bloodstained shirts, of the world's most powerful beings, I want to hold power myself."

Corbie said, "Careful, Mother. Remember, your curse brings benefits as well as frustrations."

"I know. And this is our best strategy. Burn her young every night, increase our influence every day. Then I'll give you the power I can never hold, my son. I'll give it to all my curse-hatched sons and all my curse-hatched daughters."

Corbie grinned. "It's working. We stop curses being lifted, we keep more curse-hatched alive, and soon we'll build an army that can rule the world!"

Nan nodded. "An army of curse-hatched, with you at their head and me by your side. By your side..." She sighed. "Right. Bath time and bedtime for this one."

She handed the baby to Corbie. "Start filling the bath. I need to stretch my wings."

Corbie held the baby away from his body, at arm's length.

Nan laughed. "Be quick, you know what she's like when she's not got a nappy on!"

The ragged crow carried the shining baby towards the door. Three more crows swooped from the darkness above the throne to follow him out.

Nan lifted her arms and changed into a blue bird. She flew straight up into the high rafters, then dived down to hover above the ashes of the fire.

The blue bird was slimmer and more elegant than a crow, with pale blue feathers, a bright blue beak and dark blue legs.

As Molly watched Nan soar and hover, she hoped the bird wouldn't fly between the pillars and spot them all.

The bird glided over towards the throne then flew round it, directly above a silver circle embedded in the floor a couple of metres from the padded chair. As she flew, she sang a soft sad song.

Then she settled onto the ground, outside the metal ring, and changed back into the old woman in her blue dress.

Nan smoothed her apron, then strode towards the door. "I'd better check that young crow hasn't made the bathwater too hot."

As the door closed behind Nan, Molly saw Atacama creep round the pillar and stare up at the darkness above the throne.

"No more crows." He padded over to Molly, Beth and Theo. "We're safe, for now."

Beth slumped at the base of the pillar. "Innes isn't safe. He's been captured by the curse-hatched. And he said we weren't even his friends."

Molly sat down beside her. "He said that to protect us, not because he meant it. If he meant it, he'd have told them we were behind the pillars."

"He tried to protect the baby too," said Atacama. "He was the only one of us brave enough to try to save the baby from the flames."

"That wasn't bravery, it was ignorance," said Theo. "I wasn't being cowardly when I didn't dash out to grab the Promise Keeper, I just doubted that an elemental being, even a baby one, could be hurt by a simple wood fire."

"Is that why you stopped us running out?" said Beth. "Because you knew the baby wasn't in danger?"

Theo nodded. "I'd have stopped Innes too, if I could, but perhaps it's just as well I didn't, because his impetuous act got us lots of useful information."

"It also got him captured," said Beth. "We have to rescue him right now."

Atacama said, "He'll be fine for a while. He's at a feast, what harm can come to him there?"

Theo frowned. "That depends on what he eats."

Molly said, "We can free Innes at the same time as the other curse-casters. But we can't rely on Nan to help us."

"No. She's Corbie's mum!" said Beth.

"She's the mother of all the curse-hatched." Theo sighed. "And she's caring for the Promise Keeper, who decides when curses are lifted and therefore when curse-hatched die. That explains why the helix is becoming unbalanced."

"But she seemed so nice..." said Beth.

"She's planning to use a curse-hatched army to take over the world," said Molly. "How can we stop her?"

Atacama and Theo looked at each other.

Theo said, "Her curse."

The sphinx nodded.

Theo turned to Molly and Beth. "Nan's curse might be the root of her power as well as the cause of her anger. If we can discover the terms of her curse, we can work out how to reduce her power."

Molly stood up. "It's about time a curse helped us out. Let's go and hunt for the one useful curse in this Hall."

Chapter Twenty

Night was falling outside and the corridors were deserted. "Perhaps it's everyone's bath time and bedtime," murmured Molly.

They crept into the Chamber of Promises and closed the door quietly.

"If Nan is the mother of the curse-hatched, then she's really old and her curse is probably old too," said Beth. "So we're looking for an old mirror."

Theo nodded, and pointed to carved symbols on the front of each rack. "They're filed by type of curse: transformation, burning, slow death, that sort of thing... But we don't know what type her curse is, or even what all the symbols mean."

Molly stood back and considered the racks. "I don't think we need to understand all the symbols. It looks like the oldest mirrors for each type of curse are stored at the left-hand side of the rack. Let's just look at the mirrors from that end of every rack."

As they brought over the three or four oldest mirrors

from each rack and laid them on the table, they saw people turned into snakes and wolves. They saw fabled beasts melted into puddles and frozen into ice. They saw curses cast by warring kings and terrified mice. They picked up mirrors heavy with jewels and mirrors light as a slice of air.

Then, at the back of a rack marked with a broken crown, Molly found an old mirror that was polished and well cared for. "What about this one?"

The mirror was made of gleaming black stone, with edges so thin, it was like the blade of a wide dagger.

"Obsidian!" said Theo. "That could be it."

Molly laid the mirror on the table and they all crowded round.

The shiny black surface of the mirror shimmered and they saw a young man in golden robes being dragged towards a hole in a stone floor by four shadowy creatures. He flung a cup of wine at a slim woman on a throne, then screamed panicked words at a bulkier woman in a metal dress standing by the throne. The standing woman shouted back at him and he repeated his words, more deliberately. The woman on the throne laughed as the man was pulled into the pit, which closed over his head.

The mirror misted over. Then the scene ran again. The man screaming as he was dragged away, throwing wine at the queen on the throne and throwing a curse at the warrior beside the throne.

But Molly couldn't understand the words. "It's too old. It's not in English. We don't know what he's saying."

Theo was muttering beside her, his fingers trembling on the edge of the table. The mirror misted and repeated again and again, and Theo stared at it, mumbling the words, his hands shaking even more.

"Lift it off," ordered Atacama. "Lift it off the table!"

Molly grabbed the obsidian mirror. The voices stopped. The image faded.

And Theo slid to the floor.

Beth crouched beside him, as Molly put the mirror in its rack.

When Molly came back to the table, Beth was wafting Theo's cloak over his face.

"Thanks, I'm fine," he said, pushing Beth's fanning hand away.

"Did you understand the curse?" asked Atacama.

"It was in an old Mesopotamian dialect, which I've only read, never heard, but I got the sense of it."

"Why did it affect you so much?" asked Molly. "Did you need raw power to understand it?"

"No. The armoured woman by the throne... I recognised her voice. She's the one who cursed me, the one who attacked me outside the crowgate, stole my power, shaved my head and turned me into a toad. That was Nan in her true form, in her younger original self. Nan is much more powerful than we realised."

"Is she more powerful than you?" asked Beth.

Theo ran his hand over his scarred scalp. "Right now, of course she is. But she was also more powerful when

I was at my strongest. She's an ancient being of great malevolence."

"So what is her curse?" asked Atacama. "Can we use it against her?"

Theo nodded. "Possibly. That young man was a king, being dragged to the underworld in place of his queen, who believed she was a goddess. The woman by the throne, Nan, was a minor queen and a great warrior, who served the goddess as her protector. The young king blamed Nan's manipulation and ambition for the queen turning against him. So he cursed Nan, saying she would never sit on a throne, she would never be in the supreme position of power, she must serve by the side of the throne forever..."

"Forever?" said Atacama, a purr in his voice. "Forever! What a foolish young man."

"Yes," said Theo. "That probably wasn't what he meant."

"But it's what he gave her."

"What do you two mean?" said Beth. "Stop talking in riddles."

Theo smiled. "If a curse that lasts 'forever' is strong enough, cast by someone powerful enough, it can make the 'forever' come true. The victim lives forever, so they suffer their curse eternally. That's why Nan's still here, serving reluctantly beside the throne, thousands of years later. She's been given immortality by her curse."

Atacama said, "That must be what Corbie meant by the benefits of the curse. So if we could break her curse..." The sphinx grinned.

"If her curse is broken, will she die?" asked Molly. "That's a bit brutal."

Atacama shrugged. "She's burning a baby every night to stop the baby growing up, she's imprisoning curse-casters and preventing curses being lifted. She's not a cuddly old lady. She's quite brutal herself."

"How would we break the curse?" asked Molly. "That young king didn't look like he was setting easy limits."

"He didn't build in any way to lift it," said Theo. "It was a very strong curse. And he added the power of the dark shadows dragging him down to the earliest human version of hell. It's not an easy curse to break."

"So we could end her long bitter life if we could break the curse," said Molly, "but we can't break the curse."

"We could make the curse contradict itself," said Theo. "Nan can't put herself on the throne, but if she's put there by someone else, the curse would no longer be true. Seating her on the throne might cancel out the 'forever'."

"Or it might give her all the power she's desired for millennia," said Atacama.

Theo shrugged. "That's the risk. But I can't see any other options."

"How do we put her on the throne?" asked Beth.

"Lift her, shove her, force her."

Beth frowned. "She's stronger than you, even when you have all your power. How can we force her to do anything?"

Molly said, "She doesn't know we know about her plans or the curse, so she won't be on her guard. And we have the rainbow-maker she wants. Perhaps we can trick her onto the throne."

"I have an idea to get her into the throne room," said Theo. "Once we're there, if any one of you sees a chance to get her onto that throne, grab it."

Beth snorted. "That's not a plan. It's a hope that an opportunity will present itself."

"It's the best we can do. With our four different skills and powers, we have a chance."

"We'd have a better chance with Innes," said Beth. "Can we break him out of the feast before we face Nan?"

They went to a window and peered cautiously into the courtyard.

Innes was sitting by the fountain, popping green olives into the mouth of a giggling mermaid.

"He's having fun," said Beth.

"He's closely guarded." Theo pointed at three crows circling above the kelpie's head.

Innes turned round to get more olives out of a bowl on the table, and looked over at the arched windows of the chamber. He smiled, raised his eyebrows to indicate the crows above him, then nodded once.

"He knows we're here," said Atacama. "He knows we'll get him out."

"We need him to defeat Nan," said Beth. "Innes is better than any of us in a straight fight. I know I didn't want him here, but now we know what we're up against, I don't think we can do this without him."

"We have to," said Molly. "If we help him escape, the crows will notice. Then we'd be fighting hundreds of crows as well as one old woman."

Beth sighed, then walked back to the table and picked up the wood-framed mirror that reflected Molly's curse. "When the curse is lifted, the mirror shatters. What if we broke the mirror? Would that break the curse?"

"I don't know," said Theo. "There are no records of such an experiment."

Beth handed the mirror to Molly. "Let's see if smashing it breaks your curse. Because I'm sure it's not a good idea to take on an ancient dark-magic user when you're filled with darkness yourself. You have to break it now."

Molly looked at the mirror, then at the stone floor.

She lifted the mirror above her head, then slowly lowered it again.

Molly thought about how the world looked and smelt and sounded when she was a hare. She thought about racing Innes, about the power in her legs and her speed over the earth. Then she remembered how vulnerable she felt when she stopped running.

She hadn't chosen this magical ability. But she could choose to get rid of it. She lifted the mirror high, her arm stretched above her head. She closed her eyes and threw it at the stone-flagged floor.

The mirror hit the stone.

And Molly heard a loud **CRACK**.

Chapter Twenty-One

Molly opened her eyes and looked down.

The mirror was undamaged. The flagstone on the floor was broken.

Beth sighed. "It was worth a try."

"Yes, it was. But I'll have to carry my curse for a while longer."

And they left the Chamber of Promises.

"I saw a bath in the baby's playroom," said Molly. "She's probably splashing with her duckies in there."

As they walked along the corridor, Theo said, "Let me do the talking. Molly, show her the rainbow-maker, but don't give it to her."

Theo knocked on the playroom door. **Rata-tat-tat.** Confident and loud.

"Come in," called Nan's gentle voice. "I'm just taking the baby out of the bath."

They walked in and saw Nan standing beside a big claw-footed bath. The squirming Promise Keeper was cuddled up to Nan's shoulder, wrapped in a hooded yellow towel.

Nan raised her eyebrows. "The young questors have returned. How clever and brave of you. Do you have the rainbow-maker?"

Molly pulled the crystal fang carefully out of her pocket.

Nan's wrinkled face brightened in genuine pleasure, and she reached forward.

"Not yet," said Theo. "We brought it for the baby. We can only give to it to the baby."

"But it's probably covered in germs. I'll have to wash it before she touches it."

Theo shook his head. "We have to present it to the baby."

"Nonsense," said Nan. "She's sleepy, she won't enjoy it just now. I'll take it."

Theo smiled. "My people have a tradition that quest objects must be handed over in a specific ceremony. If I don't do this right, with the appropriate words and correct ritual, I'll have to fill in piles of paperwork when I get home. So if you take us to the most ceremonial room in the building, something with height and grace and ideally a bit of gold paint, then I will speak the words for the end of a quest and Molly will hand over the rainbow-maker officially. To the baby. Then you can grab it and clean it. It will only take a few minutes, my lady." Theo yawned. "We're keen to get home."

"Just a few minutes?" asked Nan.

"Yes. Then everything will be done properly, we'll take the curse-casters away and you'll have peace and quiet."

"The throne room would be the best place, if you want

gold paint. Also, I lit a fire there earlier, so it's nice and warm. We'll go once the Keeper is dry and dressed." She pointed at Molly. "You, the holder of the rainbow-maker. Tell us the tale of your quest as our bedtime story. I'm curious to know why you've returned with one less kelpie and one more sphinx."

Molly looked at Theo. He nodded.

So as Nan dried the baby, Molly said, "After you kindly showed us the way out of the Keeper's Hall, we met up with Atacama. Then we went into the mountains, tracking a wyrm we met last week."

"Ah yes, the wrym who escaped that neat earth-binding curse." Nan wrapped a nappy round the baby's bottom. "Did you find her?"

"Yes, after a disagreement about rights of way with some grey men. We asked her if she knew where to find the snake's first toy. We thought, because she was a serpent..."

"Very clever."

"She took us to a cave, where a very old, very big, very scary black snake asked us questions and laughed at our answers. Especially when it turned out Innes – the kelpie you met last time – had cast a curse on his dad. So we got this crystal fang but we lost Innes, because he and Beth had an argument and he stormed off. Then we were attacked by nasty creatures called nuckelavee, but we managed to defeat them."

"Goodness, what an exciting bedtime story. How did you defeat them?"

"They can only come onto land once a day, so we pushed them back into the sea, and they couldn't attack us again."

Nan frowned. "I suppose every power has a weakness. Aren't they clever children?" She blew on the baby's tummy, then eased the baby's arms and legs into a pure white sleepsuit.

"Then we got home, answered the sphinx's riddle, had a chat with the mosaic men and here we are! With the rainbow-maker!" Molly held it up and smiled. She hoped she hadn't told Nan anything that would undermine Theo's plan.

"You've worked very hard." Nan picked the baby up and walked to the door. "If you want to speak the words to end your quest, we have just enough time before beddy-byes."

She led them to the pillared room, where they oohed and ahhed as if they'd never seen it before. Theo strode towards the throne, past the cold dead fire. "This is the best place."

"The best place for what?" said Nan. "What exactly are you planning, young man?"

"This ceremony simply ensures that the quest object is given to the right person. The Promise Keeper is the only baby in the room, so I'm sure she'll be the right person for a toy. But you'll have to stand away from her, Nan, so your presence doesn't confuse the ceremony. Can you seat her on the throne?"

Nan frowned and took a step back.

Theo smiled reassuringly. "Or would she be comfier on that cushion?" He pointed to the golden silk cushion on the floor, just outside the silver line.

"The cushion, definitely."

"Place her there and I'll speak the words."

Nan laid the baby on the cushion and stepped away.

Theo arranged everyone into a circle between the slab of rock and the throne: Theo standing near the slab, then, going clockwise, Molly, the baby, Nan near the foot of the throne, Atacama and Beth.

Theo put one hand into the dusty ashes and spoke.

Molly expected to hear ancient words: the words he'd spoken to the wyrm or the words he'd understood from the obsidian mirror. But Theo spoke in a language they all understood.

"We have quested. We have sought. We have discovered. Now, to end our quest, we must present our prize to the one who will most appreciate and best use its strength.

"By the power I draw from the fire that burns on this slab each night, I call on all here to reveal their true and fundamental nature. Show yourselves!"

Molly saw pale flames flicker above the ashes. Silver smoke billowed into the air and spread around the circle.

The smoke coiled round the six figures until each of them was obscured by a smoky form of themselves. But the smoky forms were not all exactly the same as the beings they were wrapped around.

Molly saw an elegant birch tree in Beth's place.

Atacama was still a sphinx.

The Promise Keeper was a shining teenager in pale robes, standing up, stretching her arms, running her fingers through her long curls.

Theo was different too. He had thick shiny hair pulled back in a plait and thick dark eyeliner round his eyes. He wore a short linen kilt round his hips and a wide beaded collar round his shoulders, and he looked healthier than she'd ever seen him.

Molly looked at her own feet, wondering if she'd see a smoky hare crouched on the floor, wondering if that was her true form. But she just saw her trainers. Then she noticed her hands. Her right hand held a shadowy version of the rainbow-maker, her left hand held a ball of vivid white light. She flexed her fingers. The light glowed brighter.

Then Molly heard a laugh.

She looked round at Nan. The little old lady in the apron was hidden by a tall smoky warrior. A younger woman with a sword in her right hand, a belt of knives and a long dress made of small metal lozenges. A woman with ringlets of glistening dark hair and even more eyeliner than Theo. She was the woman from the obsidian mirror. And she was laughing.

"A revealing spell. Very tricky. So now you know I'm not just a babysitter. Perhaps you knew that already. But you didn't know my full power, or you would never have come back."

She screamed one word and the smoke vanished. There

was no tree, no girl by the cushion, no jewelled collar on Theo, no warm light in Molly's hand.

Then Nan changed. Not into a shadowy shape, but into a real solid armoured warrior, with real solid weapons.

"How dare you reveal me like that, boy? I am Ninshibur and I eat desert magicians for breakfast. I've defeated you before. I stole your power and your pretty plait. Didn't you learn your lesson? Now that you see who I am, you see who should really hold the rainbow-maker. Give it to me, girl."

"No," said Molly. "It's not for you."

The warrior shrugged. "Then give it to the baby. I'll just take it from her. She'll never grow up enough to sit on the throne. I will stand beside it and rule everything, through my children."

She laughed again. "I know I don't look like a mother, but I have *thousands* of children. Not this weak baby, she's just my job, but my darling curse-hatched children, hatched from the stone eggs my bird-form laid over centuries. My children feed on curses, on the spells of the evil and the foolish, those chased by dreams of revenge and anger. What better food for those who want to rule the world!

"I am a queen! Yet I have been condemned to stand forever at the side of the throne, to be a handmaiden, a cupbearer, a bodyguard, a nurse. Eventually I decided that if I couldn't hold true power myself, I would hold it through my children. But my army didn't grow fast enough, so we protected the curses. Now our numbers grow, and soon my children will be both birds and soldiers, in a curse-driven army.

"But you irritating brats have been interfering, lifting curses and trying to free the curse-casters. And you failed to die on that quest. So now you can give me the crystal fang I've always desired, then join my curse-casters at that endless feast. Give me the rainbow-maker and bow down to me!"

"Why would we bow to someone who isn't even on a throne?" said Theo.

Nan screamed in frustration and raised her sword.

Theo smiled. "You're not sneaking up behind me now. I'm ready for you." He circled his hands. His cloak whirled and disintegrated and became a vortex of sand.

He flicked the spinning cone towards Nan.

She slashed her sword through the whirling sand and it dropped dustily to the floor.

She shook her head. "I've learnt a lot of magic in five thousand years, and I've concentrated on the ugly oozy dark magic. Your dry desert magic doesn't impress me. And I can do circles too." She drew a small circle with her index finger.

The sand whirled upwards again, not into the wide cone of a whirlwind, but into the tight cord of a rope.

The rope of sand whipped over to Theo, wrapped round his neck and hoisted him into the air. He dangled from the rope, coughing and choking.

"Too tight?" Nan smiled. "Let's make your neck smaller."

Theo turned from a boy into a piglet.

Then from the piglet into a skunk.

And from the skunk into a rat.

Each time, the noose got smaller so the rope stayed tight round his neck.

Theo turned from a rat into a familiar toad.

From the toad into a newt.

From the newt into a worm.

And from the worm into a cockroach.

"Not so handsome now, are you?" said Nan.

And Theo stayed a cockroach, suspended from a thin string of golden sand.

Molly wasn't sure if she should run at Nan to attack her, or hide the rainbow-maker first so she didn't take it nearer to Nan.

As Molly hesitated, Beth screamed, "That's cruel. Leave him alone," and ran toward the pile of firewood.

Atacama leapt towards Nan, who pulled five daggers from her belt and threw them at the sphinx in a tight formation, like a clawed hand. Atacama fell to the floor, with five long wounds in his side.

Beth flung the entire pile of fragrant firewood at Nan. A wall of wood crashed through the air towards the warrior.

Nan flicked her hand. The firewood swerved around her in a smooth arc, and flew back towards Beth. Beth raised her arms, but the wood hit her with a crunch, knocked her down and collapsed on top of her.

The baby made a small sleepy noise and waved her fists in the air.

Molly looked round.

Atacama was lying on the floor, bleeding. Beth was buried under a pile of wood. Theo was dangling from a noose in the air, six insect legs waving feebly.

Molly stood on her own, facing the warrior queen.

Nan smiled at her. "Let's start again, Molly. You are a simple human girl, with no power of your own. Be sensible, give me that rainbow-maker, then bow down to me."

Molly nodded.

She ducked under Theo's choking form, walked past the firewood burying Beth, stepped over Atacama's bleeding body.

And she held the rainbow-maker up towards the warrior.

Chapter
Twenty-two

Molly pointed the sharp end of the rainbow-maker at Nan.

She had no idea what the rainbow-maker could do. The ancient snake had warned them of its power, the nuckelavee had attacked them for it, this warrior queen had sent them on a quest for it. So the crystal fang probably did something. But what? How did it work? And would it be helpful or would it be dangerous?

With all her friends held prisoner, injured or slowly choking, Molly didn't think that whatever the rainbow-maker did could make things worse.

She remembered the flash of light from the sharp end of the fang when she held it up to the sun on the beach. She angled the fang so the wide base pointed at the glowing fire, and a bright beam of striped light shot out of the tip and bounced beautifully around the throne room.

Nan laughed, the segments of her armoured dress shaking and rattling. "You have no idea how to use it! Give it to me."

Over the clinking of the metal dress, Molly heard a soft wooden clunking from her right. The pile of wood over Beth was moving slightly.

Molly kept the base of the rainbow-maker pointed at the flames and aimed the tip directly at the firewood. The logs lit up, shimmering violet indigo blue green yellow orange red. The logs rolled and split, then slid off Beth, who stood up, brushing splinters from her hair.

The rainbow-lit wood chips shivered and fell apart into a heap of sawdust, which rippled into a stack of creamy sheets of paper.

Molly turned and aimed the rainbow at Theo. She hoped to shake the rope of sand apart, but the rope held. However, the cockroach shook and jerked, and turned into a worm, then a newt, then a toad, then a rat, then a skunk, then a piglet…

Finally, red-faced and coughing, Theo the boy was hanging from the end of the expanded noose again. And his toes were just touching the ground, so he could support himself and take the pressure off his throat.

Molly moved the rainbow-maker towards Nan.

Nan shook her head. "The rainbow-maker is an instrument of creation. But it must destroy before it creates. Just as a prism rips a beam of light apart to create a rainbow, that fang tears objects apart to create something new and beautiful. It's risky to use it on your friends, and you lack the courage to use it on me."

Molly started to lift the rainbow-maker.

And the door to the throne room opened with a **CRASH**.

Innes rushed in. "Are you alright? When I heard Beth scream, I couldn't pretend to be happy at that feast any longer."

A flock of crows screeched through the door after him.

Beth walked round the pile of paper. "Thanks for bringing us more enemies to fight."

Molly looked at Theo, the impossible noose tightening round his neck. She sliced through the golden rope with the sharp point of the crystal and the sand fell in grains to the floor.

Theo collapsed.

The sand glimmered and melted into a scattering of diamond-shaped panes of glass.

Molly turned back to Nan, who was standing in front of the throne with a pillar of crows whirling above her.

"I do have the courage to use this rainbow-maker," said Molly, "if it's the only way to save my friends. Do you have the courage to face it? It destroyed wood and created paper. It destroyed sand and created glass. If it destroyed you and your crows, what would it create? Feather dusters?"

She started to aim the rainbow-maker again.

Nan yelled, "Crows! Bring me that fang and bring those children to their knees."

The crows swooped down, pecking and scratching and battering Molly. She hunched her shoulders and lifted her left hand to protect her eyes. She was suddenly aware that Innes was beside her, trying to shelter her, in his horse form.

Molly knew they were fortunate that the rainbow-maker had only destroyed each animal shape of Theo and re-created his previous shape. If she pointed it at a living being again, what would it destroy and what would it create? Did she want to find out?

She stepped nearer the fire and called to Nan, "I will use this, unless you and your crows leave the Keeper's Hall right now."

She held the rainbow-maker up. As soon as she raised it, the crows mobbing her veered away.

The baby lying on the cushion giggled and waved at the crows flocking above her.

Molly aimed the base of the fang at the flames and the tip into the air. The whole room lit up, with ribbons of light curving up and swirling down. As the rainbows danced, the throne room started to shake. The pillars, the rafters, the stone floor.

The building trembled.

Molly put her hand over the base. The light stopped flowing and the Hall steadied.

She pointed the tip at Nan again, keeping the base covered. "Leave, now. Leave the Promise Keeper alone and let her grow up."

"I will not leave. I've put centuries of work into this plan." Nan raised her sword, aiming it at Molly.

Molly gritted her teeth and took her hand away, letting light flow into the rainbow-maker and out towards Nan.

Nan lit up like a Christmas tree. The warrior queen

began to shiver. Her dress quivered and rattled. Lozenges of metal, lit up like coloured sequins, were shaken free and fell to the ground. As they landed, they melted into shiny coins with an ancient queen's head.

Nan jerked and became the old woman in the apron again. She shuddered and her blue dress started to become blue feathers. "NO!" she screamed. "I will not be destroyed. I have been cursed with *forever*!"

Molly saw Nan clench her jaws and fight the shaking. Then Nan dragged herself back, by pure will and vast ambition, into the form of the warrior queen. She screeched at her crows to defend her and not to retreat this time.

Molly heard Corbie's distant voice, also yelling orders, as he ran into the throne room.

And the crows attacked again.

Crows landed on Molly's arm and pecked at her fingers. Molly couldn't hold the rainbow-maker steady between the fire and Nan. She wrapped both hands round the crystal to keep it safe from attacking beaks.

Dozens of birds surrounded her, grabbing her hair and clothes. Innes reared and kicked beside her, but he was wearing a moving coat of crows. Atacama and Theo lay on the ground, with triumphant birds perched on them. Molly glimpsed Beth cowering behind the throne.

The weight of the crows forced Molly to her knees.

Nan yelled. "Hold her still, so I can claim the rainbow-maker for myself."

Molly, held immobile by a hundred birds, watched this ruthless warrior stretch out to seize an object with the power of destruction and creation. She couldn't let Nan have it.

Molly shouted, "Innes!" She opened her fingers and dropped the rainbow-maker onto the stone floor, under the horse.

Who lifted a hoof and stamped on the crystal fang.

The rainbow-maker flew into a thousand pieces, as if it had been waiting for its own destruction all these years.

Nan screamed, "No!"

Corbie said, "Mother, it's fine. We don't need it. We're building an army. The rainbow-maker was a bonus, when you had willing children to quest for it, but we don't need it."

"But I wanted the power! I *never* get to hold the power!"

"We will have more power, stronger power, power we build ourselves."

Molly sighed. She'd stopped Nan getting the rainbow-maker, but now she had nothing to defend herself or her friends against the crows forcing her to the floor and the anger of this furious warrior.

Then Molly saw Beth stand up. Beth hadn't been cowering behind the throne: she'd been making a weapon. She'd sharpened a stray bit of firewood into a short spear, which she threw straight at Nan.

An arrow of crows flew across the throne room and crashed into the spear, knocking it off course, so it bounced against Nan's arm rather than striking her in the heart.

Nan looked at the graze on her wrist. "Ouch."

Then she walked round the edge of the silver circle towards Beth, who was standing behind the throne. "You won't get the chance to bow to me, dryad, unless you can bow without a head!" Nan raised her sword.

Molly yelled, "No!"

She slid out of the claws of the crows, sprinted towards Nan, and leapt at her.

She hit Nan's ankles.

The warrior queen tripped and fell forward.

She fell across the silver circle marked on the floor.

She fell towards the throne.

Molly looked up as Nan fell down, and Molly realised she was seeing the world in widescreen, from ground level. She was a hare.

She couldn't remember growling. But this had been the only way to escape the crows, the only way to catch up with Nan, the only way to save Beth.

Molly crouched at the edge of the circle and saw Nan twist and fall onto the wide velvet seat of the throne.

Nan sat on the throne.

Nan smiled.

Then she crumbled. She shrank and dried and faded until she wasn't there at all.

As Nan faded away, Molly heard a whisper. "At last, I can stop wanting it. At last..."

Chapter Twenty-three

Molly heard shock and anger in the wails of the curse-hatched, as they watched their mother vanish.

She knew her hare form would be useless in a fight, and she'd noticed a hare-sized hiding place under the throne, so she leapt over the silver line.

As she landed she felt her bones fizz and buckle, and she collapsed onto the floor. She closed her eyes, not wanting to watch herself melt. She felt her body struggle to change and for several uncomfortable breaths she was stuck between hare and girl.

Then she felt the weight of trainers on her feet and jeans tight round her legs. She opened her eyes. She was a girl again.

The crows were still screaming, their high rough calls echoing round the rafters. *Krah-ah-ah-ah!*

Innes stood in his boy form beside Molly and hauled her to her feet. He held Molly's hand up in the air, like she'd won a boxing match. "Here's the one who disintegrated and defeated Nan. Here she is!"

"Thanks," muttered Molly, "make *me* the target."

"Here's the girl with even more power than your mother! Who dares take her on?"

"I dare," croaked Corbie, tears running down his cheeks as he stepped forward.

But he was the only one. The rest of the crows were flying out of the throne room, swooping into the corridor, knocking each other out of the air in their haste to get away from Molly.

When Corbie saw his army retreating, he shifted to crow-form and flapped unevenly after them.

The room fell silent.

Innes let go of Molly and ran to Atacama. He skidded on the stone floor and stumbled to a stop beside the motionless sphinx.

Molly looked round at Beth, who was staring at the empty throne. Then at Theo, who was lying flat on the floor, but gasping and therefore breathing. So she ran to Atacama too.

When she got there, Atacama's eyes were open. Innes was saying, "But what happened to you?"

"She threw knives at him," said Molly. "Five knives, five wounds."

"Five claws," said Atacama quietly.

"Let me see," said Innes.

"No!" Atacama sat up carefully, twisted his spine and neck, and looked at his side. Then he licked each wound once. "The scratches aren't too deep."

"We should clean them," said Innes. "We should get treatment for them." He put his hand on Atacama's back.

The sphinx hissed. Innes pulled his hand away.

"Don't touch me! Cats heal themselves. If anyone," he glared at Innes, "if *anyone* suggests taking me to a vet, I'll bite their hand off."

Molly said, "I want to check on Theo, if you're alright here?"

Atacama nodded and licked his wounds again.

Molly ran over to Theo. Beth was already there, crouched down beside him, her heavy black boots splintering the glass diamonds.

Theo was conscious too, coughing and rubbing his throat.

"Are you ok?" asked Molly.

"I will be, once I catch my breath." His voice was hoarse. "Thanks to you for destroying that rope."

"And thanks to Innes for destroying the rainbow-maker," said Molly. "Nan would have been even scarier with that in her hands."

Innes joined them. "You weren't very clear though, were you? You just dropped it under my hooves. I wasn't sure if crushing it was the right thing to do."

"It was perfect," said Beth. "You always know what the right thing is. Sometimes you even do it." She smiled at him. "Did you enjoy your curse-caster feast?"

"Not really. It won't be hard to persuade the guests to leave, once I show them what they've been eating."

Atacama walked over, slowly.

"So how exactly did you defeat Nan?" asked Innes. "Is that throne a powerful weapon?"

"No," said Theo. "She was cursed to stand beside the throne forever. And that 'forever' was giving her a very frustrating immortality."

Atacama added, "When she sat on the throne, the curse contradicted itself and she lost her 'forever'."

Beth said, "I heard her whisper something when she sat down. Did you hear it too, Molly?"

Molly nodded.

"I think she was grateful to you."

Molly sighed. "Did I kill her? Was that what happened? I didn't mean to. I was just trying to save Beth."

"But you shifted into a hare to do it," said Beth. "You have to stop shapeshifting."

"Don't nag her," said Innes. "She saved your life."

"She saved the balance of the helix too," said Theo.

"We're not finished yet," said Atacama. "We need to free the curse-casters."

"And we need to find someone to look after the baby," said Beth.

They looked at the Promise Keeper, lying quietly on the golden cushion, gazing at the ceiling.

"Where are her mum and dad?" asked Beth.

"She doesn't have parents," said Theo. "Like you were born from a tree, she was born from the earth. She needs a guardian, though ideally not another power-crazed ancient warrior. Who can care for her?" He looked round them all.

Innes laughed. "Don't look at me. I don't do babies."

Atacama said, "I only do kittens, and even then, just the fun tail-chasing bits, not litter-tray training."

"I'm better with buds and leaves," said Beth.

Molly said, "Theo, you know lots about the Keeper's Hall and you want to find out more. Why don't you stay here, while the baby grows up?"

"No, I'm too powerful."

Innes snorted. "Show off."

"When my hair grows and I can store power again, I'll be back to full strength. If I stayed here, I'd probably unbalance the helix again."

Molly sighed. "I'm back at school soon, so I can't babysit either. But we can't leave her here on her own." She walked over, picked the baby up and gave her a cuddle. "Once we've got everyone out of the Hall, we'll find a safer childminder."

They left the throne room, Molly carrying the baby. She was heavier and harder than Molly had expected, more like a porcelain doll than a cuddly toy. But she wriggled happily in Molly's arms.

Innes marched out of the nearest archway, into the courtyard.

The mermaid cooed, "Ooh, my charming water-horse, do feed me more olives..."

"They weren't olives." He raised his voice, "Nothing on these tables is what it seems."

Everyone in the courtyard turned to look at him.

"You haven't been eating olives or grapes or sushi or chocolate. You haven't been eating your favourite things. This is enchanted food, designed to keep you quiet and passive. And the curse-hatched didn't bother to enchant expensive food for you. *This* is what you've been eating."

Innes yanked the white tablecloth off the nearest table.

He wasn't attempting a magic trick. He didn't leave all the crockery sitting neatly on the table. Bowls, plates and glasses crashed to the floor and their contents spilled out. As Innes walked round the courtyard, dragging more tablecloths off, the food transformed into:

SLUGS

TWIGS   GRAVEL

SPIDERS

MUD

BRUSSEL SPROUTS

Innes called out, "You weren't invited here as a reward, or for your safety. You were brought here to increase the crows' strength by being too dozy to lift your curses. You've been prisoners, fed on rubbish. Now it's time to go home."

Most of the guests were yawning and looking around in surprise. Some were spitting out food.

The mermaid said, "What horrid crows. What nasty food. I want to go back to my seabed now. Who will carry me?"

"How can we get them out?" said Beth. "We don't know where the door will appear next."

Atacama pointed at the other side of the courtyard. "Is that it?"

Molly looked at the newly appeared door. "The carvings and pillars fit on that wall, like a jigsaw piece in the right place. But will it stay there long enough for us to get everyone out?"

Theo nodded. "That must be the door's original place. Nan's magic kept it moving, to deny the guests a way out. But now she's d—" he glanced at Molly. "Now she's gone, the door has settled back into its proper place."

Innes yelled, "Right everyone. Up and out. Back to real food and your own lives!"

Most of the guests stood up and stretched.

Beth strode across the courtyard and flung the door open. Molly followed and stood beside the doorway, with the Promise Keeper in her arms. The baby made bubbly noises and waved as the guests left.

The giant ducked under the lintel with the mermaid in his arms.

"Careful!" she screeched. "Don't drop me!"

Beth said to each guest as they left, "If you're grateful to us for releasing you, please lift the curse you cast."

The boy with the deer's legs nodded. "I will lift my

curse. It was cast in a moment of anger and I've regretted it ever since."

But several other guests shrugged or scowled as they left.

The last guest to leave was Mr Crottel, with two yawning dogs at his heels. Beth moved to stand in his way, joined suddenly by Theo, Innes and Atacama. Molly stepped back, embarrassed to see them all confront her curse-caster for her.

Beth said, "We've released you from this prison. In return, you must release our friend Molly Drummond from her curse."

Mr Crottel picked his teeth with his long yellow pinkie nail. "I liked it here. My dogs were happy, I was happy. The food tasted fine. I owe you resentment, not gratitude, for forcing me out of a free feast I was enjoying. And I won't lift her curse. She deserved it. I won't lift it and you can't make me. Let me past."

No one moved.

"What about the changes to my curse?" asked Molly. "How did that happen?"

Mr Crottel grinned. "The crows wanted revenge on someone for Corbie's clipped wing, and you were the only one still cursed. They promised me an endless feast, if I'd adjust your curse to make it more… inconvenient. So in this Hall filled with curse-casters, I found enough dark magical energy to adjust the rules and make it harder for you to shift back."

He pulled the thorny black rose from his lapel.

"But the adjustments won't hold, now the dark-magic users have dispersed." The black rose was wilting in his fingers. "What a shame."

Molly thought of all the dangers her friends had faced to give her this one chance to confront her curse-caster. And she stepped out in front of Mr Crottel.

"Lift the whole curse," she demanded. "This wasn't a party, it was a prison. It wasn't a feast, it was mud and spiders. We've freed you, so you have to free me."

"No, I don't have to do anything. It's a perfectly good curse. The adjustments were fun while they lasted..." he watched black petals drift to the ground, "...but the basic curse is yours for ever! It's not wise for a dark-magic user to lift a curse, it makes us look weak. If your friends don't let me past, or if you keep nagging me to lift the curse, I will search for enough power to make your curse worse again, now I've been shown how. So, out of my way!"

He barged between Theo and Innes, and led his dogs down the mosaic corridor.

Molly sighed. "He's not grateful. So I'll be cursed forever."

Chapter Twenty-four

Molly watched Mr Crottel slouch along the corridor and heard him snap at the mosaic men to move out of his way.

She looked down at the withered black petals. "Does that mean my curse is back to normal and I'll become a girl again when I cross ordinary boundaries as well as magical ones?"

"You can't check here," said Theo. "There are no human boundaries in the Hall. We can experiment when we get out."

"We're not going to experiment on Molly!" said Beth.

"Not yet, anyway," said Innes. "We have to find the keys to free Mrs Sharpe. Let's search the rooms."

They split up: Beth and Atacama going through one archway; Molly, Innes and Theo taking another.

"Anyone else want to carry the baby?" asked Molly. "She's a bit heavy."

Theo and Innes acted like they hadn't heard, and the baby smiled up at her. So she snuggled the baby more comfortably in her arms, and followed them into the first room.

It was a kitchen, filled with piles of rotting muddy food. They looked along the shelves and checked the drawers, but they didn't find any keys.

Further along the corridor, they checked a cupboard full of tablecloths, a smelly toilet with lots of different-sized cubicles, and the Chamber of Promises. Then they opened the playroom door.

As Innes and Theo started looking through the toys, Molly put the baby in her cot and searched drawers of towels and blankets, many of them embroidered with stars and the name Estelle.

Then she realised Theo was standing still, staring at something.

"Have you found them?"

"What?"

"Have you found the keys?"

Theo shook his head. He was staring at the shelf of dolls.

"Keep searching," said Innes. "Or can't toads keep up with horses and hares?"

Theo didn't answer.

Molly walked over to him. "What is it?"

"She kept it. The old fool kept it. I could have reclaimed it the first time we were here!"

"What did she keep?"

Theo reached up to the most beautiful doll on the shelf. A dark-skinned black-eyed many-armed doll in a bright red sari, with a thick black plait hanging over her shoulder.

He tugged the plait and it fell into his hand. It wasn't part of the doll; it had just been wrapped round the toy's neck.

"This is my plait. She didn't burn it. She didn't destroy all the power I'd gathered and stored!" He grinned at Molly. "I wish I'd had this when we met the grey men and the nuckelavee, and when we confronted Nan in the throne room."

Innes said, "You managed fine with the grey men and the nuckelavee. And Molly dealt with Nan in the throne room."

Theo let the plait hang down from his hand. It almost reached the floor.

"Didn't you ever cut your hair?" asked Molly.

He shook his head. "This is a dozen years' worth of power. I won't let it go again." He coiled it up and put it in his pocket.

"I don't think the keys are in here," said Innes, looking round the cluttered room. "We can search more thoroughly later, if we don't find them anywhere else."

Molly picked up the baby and they tried the next room. It looked like a staffroom for the curse-hatched guards, with tables, chairs, wooden perches, a few black feathers and a bunch of rusty keys hanging from a nail.

They ran outside and Innes yelled, "We've got the keys!"

Beth and Atacama emerged from an archway. As they all headed towards the tallest tower, Molly shifted the baby from one arm to the other. "She's getting heavier..."

They entered the room with the round cages.

Mrs Sharpe peered through the bars. "Young sphinx, you're injured."

"Just scratches," he said. "And it was worth it to drive the crows out of the Hall."

A golden lizard in a nearby cage snapped, "Are you going to let us out?"

Innes unlocked the round cages. Most of the prisoners – two-legged, four-legged, six-legged and eight-legged – rushed out, then grew or shrank or changed shape or flicked fire from their fingers.

Mrs Sharpe simply stretched. "It's nice to be out of that circle. It was cramping my style."

She walked over to Molly. "Have you been left holding the baby?"

Molly looked down. The Promise Keeper was asleep in her arms. "She's quite sweet really. Nan was keeping her artificially young, burning her back to a newborn every night."

"Poor wee thing." Mrs Sharpe took the baby from Molly and stroked her white cheek.

"She has no one to look after her now," said Molly. "Would you stay and take care of her, Mrs Sharpe?"

"Me? I have crops to plant! I can't stay at the Keeper's Hall for years while this one grows up."

Theo said, "Her natural growth has been held back for centuries, so she'll probably grow to adulthood in a few months. She just needs someone with wisdom and kindness to guide her while she learns her role and while the helix regains its balance."

Mrs Sharpe laid her hand on the baby's bouncy gold

curls. She smiled. "I suppose her naptime would give me peace and quiet to try a few new knitting patterns. And she looks like a lovely little girl. I'll stay for a while, but not past springtime."

Theo said, "Thank you. Now, we must shut the crowgate, so the Keeper can't be influenced by the curse-hatched crows again while she's still so young."

Innes and Beth were showing the final prisoners out of the arched door, Beth making her usual request that they lift the curses they'd cast. Theo and Atacama strolled over to join them.

Molly said, "Mrs Sharpe, can I ask you a quick question about my curse?"

"Of course, my dear."

"It's convenient sometimes, changing into a hare. But Beth thinks the dark magic is rotting my inner core. So, am I damaging myself or making myself a bad person, by choosing to shift and even enjoying it?"

Mrs Sharpe looked up from the sleeping baby. "Dryads are suspicious of any magic that isn't nature magic. They call almost everything else dark magic. But whether magic is good or bad isn't about where the magic comes from, it's about what you do with it. If you can find joy in a curse or, even better, use the curse to help people, then you're turning dark magic to light. That's not harming you. Becoming a hare unexpectedly isn't safe if you meet a fox or a hound or a hunter with a gun. But the shift itself isn't doing you any damage at all."

Molly grinned. Then she wondered whether Mrs Sharpe could explain the bright light she'd seen in her left hand, in the throne room. "What would it mean if a revealing spell—?"

But she heard her friends walking back across the courtyard. Theo was saying, "If Molly saw them fly into this tower earlier, the crowgate's inner door must be at the top."

So she just smiled at Mrs Sharpe and said, "Never mind. Thanks!" and ran to join her teammates.

They climbed the winding stairs to a round dusty room at top of the tower.

The empty room had just one window: a huge horizontal slit, like a letterbox, curving around the wall of the tower. There were massive metal shutters open at either side of the window, with complex hinges holding them to the wall, and heavy latches and chains to secure them.

Beth said, "It's wide enough to let a dozen birds in at once."

"It's the same shape as the crowgate back in Speyside," said Theo. "So let's close it."

"Wait," said Atacama. "They haven't all left." The sphinx was staring at the rafters of the tower's pointed roof.

A black shape plummeted towards him, aiming for his eyes.

Atacama slashed out with his claws and the crow swerved away. It perched above the window on a wide ledge, which was white with crusty bird droppings on top of smooth marble.

Theo said, "We won't harm you if you leave now and don't come back. Tell Corbie that his crows are banned from the Keeper's Hall, and that he must stop interfering in curses. Tell him I will be keeping an eye on him."

The crow changed into a skinny girl in a ragged black jacket, crouching on the ledge, "You'll be keeping an eye on him? Your own eye? You might regret that! But I'll tell him."

She somersaulted forward and fell headfirst out of the wide window.

Then they saw a crow fly up, swoop towards a dark line cutting across the sky, and vanish when she reached the line.

Theo said, "That's the crowgate leading to Speyside. I must close them both, to protect the baby Promise Keeper as she grows up."

Theo took the glossy black plait out of his pocket and laid it round his neck.

He blew out of the window, one gentle puff of breath, as if he was blowing fluff off a sleeve. As he blew, Molly heard a flurry of wind brush the outside of the tower.

Theo counted quietly, "Three, two, one…"

Then they saw the dark slit in the sky narrow and close, and heard a distant thudding slam.

Theo smiled, then said, "Take three steps backwards, please. Fast!"

As they all moved into the middle of the round room, a gust of wind blew into the tower and started to whirl round the circular wall, getting faster and faster and stronger and stronger.

Molly could see it picking up dusty feathers from the edge of the floor, whipping them along and ripping them to shreds. But in the centre of the room, just a few steps away, her hair was barely ruffled by a breeze.

The wind raced round and round, gaining momentum and speed. Then in one howling burst it slammed both shutters closed with a crash like thunder and sparks like lightning.

Molly ducked away from the storm of noise and light. When the wind died down and the echoes quietened, she looked up. The shutters were no longer shutters. The hinges were gone, the latches and chains were gone. The window was sealed with one smooth solid curved piece of metal.

Theo, who was now lighting the room with a pale yellow flame floating above his left hand, put the plait back in his pocket and nodded. "There's no longer a crowgate leading from Speyside to the Keeper's Hall. So my mission is complete. I can return to my family now, tell them what caused the imbalance and that I've fixed it. If I choose to admit that I was transformed into a toad—"

"And a skunk and a worm and a rat," added Innes.

Theo grinned. "If I choose to tell them that, it will be from a position of strength, having completed my mission, rather than a position of weakness, asking for help to fix my mistakes. But I'm in no rush to have that conversation with them, so I'll keep you all company a little longer. You've done a lot for me; I may be able to help you."

Innes picked up a broken black feather and pulled it apart. "No one can help me with my dad's curse. And he'll be released from the stone for the first time today, so I'd better go up to the moors and talk to him."

"We'll come with you," said Molly.

"I don't need you," he muttered. "I can do this myself."

"Of course you can," she said. "But we'll come anyway, just in case."

They said a cheerful goodbye to Mrs Sharpe and the Promise Keeper, and a wary goodbye to the mosaic men in the corridor.

Then they stepped through the outer door into the chilly brightness of a Scottish sunrise.

"You've missed a busy night," said Caracorum calmly. "Dozens of magic users came out of the door. Was that your doing, Atacama?"

He smiled. "Perhaps I'll explain later, if you feel brave enough to show a little bit of curiosity about what we guard."

As they walked away from the door, Molly said, "I suppose I'd better shift into a hare then cross a non-magical boundary, to see if my curse really has gone back to normal."

Beth said, "You don't have to! You could just decide not to shapeshift, ever again. Then it won't matter if Mr Crottel's worsening has crumbled or not."

"That makes no sense, Beth. I don't just choose to change, remember. When I hear a dog bark or growl, I change whether I want to or not, and if I don't know how to change back I could get into real trouble. There won't be many magical boundaries in Edinburgh, for example."

"You'd be surprised," murmured Theo.

"I need to know if the curse has gone back to its original form. I need to know which boundaries will work. And I need to know if I'll shift back fast or slow. So I'm going to try it now."

"Good plan," said Innes. "Why don't we race to—"

"No. This is not a game," said Molly. "I need to do this, but I'm taking the risk that if the curse hasn't returned to normal, I might never change back."

Molly didn't want to look at Beth's pale worried face. So she turned her back on her friends.

She growled.

And she shifted into a hare, fast and hot, sudden and perfect, just like she always did.

As Molly darted between her friends' feet and paws, then sprinted towards the gate between the cooperage yard and the public road, she wondered if she'd just shifted shape for the last time.

And she wondered what grass tasted like.

Chapter Twenty-five

Molly ran. And she loved it. But she was terrified too. Terrified of all the predators that wanted to chase her, catch her, rip her and eat her, in this tiny tasty vulnerable form. Terrified of a slow change, of her body struggling between two shapes. And terrified of waiting, over the boundary, for a change that might never come.

She jumped onto the road.

And landed, hard, on her hands and knees.

Molly had never been so glad to feel grit graze her hands.

She scrambled back onto the pavement, and saw her friends running slowly towards her. She grinned and ran towards them just as slowly, on two long clumsy legs.

"It worked! I shifted back at a human boundary, and I shifted fast! Thanks so much for helping me return my curse to normal."

Everyone was smiling. Everyone except Beth.

"Your curse isn't normal. No curse is normal. You still need to get rid of the original curse."

"Yeah, well. Not today. Today we're going to help Innes talk to his dad."

They left Craigvenie and climbed into the hills. Atacama and Theo chatted about ancient scrolls. Molly and Beth discussed how trees feel about autumn. Innes didn't say much at all.

"Where exactly is your dad?" asked Molly, as they reached the top of another small heathery hill.

"He's trapped in a pool about a mile to the west of Stone Egg Wood," said Innes, "so we aren't that far away." His steps were getting slower and slower, as if he was wading through deep snow or soft sand.

"What are you going to say to him?" asked Beth. "What are you going to do?"

"Aren't *you* going to tell me exactly what I should do, with lots of detailed descriptions of how rotten I am inside?"

Beth sighed. "No. I'm going to support you whatever you decide. That's what friends are for."

"Even if you think I'm doing something wrong or daft or *dark*?"

"Then I'd support you, and also nag you just a little to change your mind."

Innes managed a small smile. "That sounds more like it." He took a deep breath, and started to stride ahead.

The others followed.

Soon, Molly heard the sound of water rushing over rocks ahead. Fast water, falling water.

Then she was falling.

They were all falling. Together.

Into a pit.

The heather gave way under them and they all fell into a deep hole. They hit the soft floor together, in a heap, the thin layer of heather that had hidden the pit falling on top of them.

Molly stood up, looked at the dark walls around them and started to say, "What—?"

Then the walls closed in.

But it couldn't be the walls that were moving. Because walls don't have eyes.

A ring of bright eyes had appeared, all round the pit, then moved in closer.

Molly and her friends were surrounded by people in dark clothing, with mud on their faces. People who had opened their eyes and stepped forward.

As Molly was grabbed by lots of hands, she heard a thud and a moan behind her.

Then a man in a crow-black coat wrapped a rope round Molly's wrists, tying her hands in front of her. Beside him, Molly recognised the thin girl from the tower.

The crow-girl leant forward and whispered, "This rope is elastic. It will hold you even if you shift to a hare. So don't bother trying to escape."

A dark shadow swooped down, grabbed Molly's shoulders in huge hard claws, then lifted her out of the pit. The giant bird dropped her onto the ground between the pit and the river.

She was still surrounded. There was a circle of black-clad people with fringed sleeves around her, and above her swooped a ring of gleaming crows. Molly struggled to her knees, her tied hands making movement awkward.

She felt wings beating behind her and twisted round. The giant crow had lifted Innes out of the pit too. He was struggling and yelling in frustration, as the bird threw him to the ground.

"The rope's elastic," he called to Molly, "there's no point getting bigger or smaller."

"I know," said Molly quietly.

The bird rose out of the pit again and dropped Theo on the ground. He was limp, and blood trickled from a new cut on his bare scalp. The curse-hatched knew he was the most powerful. They'd knocked him unconscious already.

The bird dropped Beth next. She curled up, hiding her face.

None of them spoke now. There wasn't anything to say.

Atacama fell to the ground, wrapped in rope, but still hissing and spitting.

Then a cloud of crows flew out of the pit and joined the crowd around the captives.

Molly watched one glossy crow turn into the girl from the tower and the giant crow turn into a tall dark-haired woman. They stood beside a man in a ragged black coat.

Corbie.

He smiled. "Here you all are. Just as we expected. On your way to lift another curse. We can't allow that."

"I wasn't definitely going to lift it," said Innes.

"You certainly won't lift it now. None of you will ever destroy another curse."

"Can we kill them all?" asked one of the skinnier curse-hatched, wiping mud off his spotty face.

"No, you can't kill them *all*." Corbie hauled Molly to her feet.

"We can't kill this one, because her curse keeps one of our babies alive. But she won't get away unscarred.

"Our mother is dead. You will all suffer for that. And this meddling magician said he'd keep his eye on me. So every single one of you will lose your eyes to our crows' beaks. Then four of you will lose your fingers and our younger hungrier crows will dig into your still-living bellies. After that there won't be much left of you at all.

"This girl here," he shook Molly's arm, "will only lose her eyes. And we won't peck deep into her skull, so she'll live."

Corbie stared down at Molly. "This is why you will live, girl." He held up a tiny fluffy bird. "This is your curse-hatched, growing stronger every day on the power of the curse that torments you."

The last time Molly had seen this baby bird it had been pink skin and bone, with a hare marked on its wing. It was already growing downy black feathers.

She glanced over at her friends, laid out in a line. She saw Theo twitch on the ground. She held out her hands to Corbie. "May I hold the bird?"

"Why would I trust you with one of our babies?"

Molly smiled. "I won't hurt your baby bird. I like my curse. I like being a hare. I won't hurt this wee one, because it's a symbol of my speed and freedom. May I hold my curse-hatched?"

Corbie grinned. "A victim who loves her curse! That's always amusing. Here."

He gave her the bird. Molly held it cupped between her bound hands, and stroked the soft fluffy chick with her thumb.

It squeaked at her, she smiled at it.

"I must let you live," said Corbie, "so this bird can live. But I'll also let you keep your eyes, if you promise you'll never try to kill your curse or your curse-hatched again."

"I'll happily promise that, when the time is right. First, can I choose the order in which these curse-breakers will die?"

Corbie laughed. "The darkness of the curse is working on you beautifully. But why do you want to choose that?"

Molly looked at the four figures lying on the ground. Theo furthest away, then Innes, then Atacama, then Beth almost at her feet. "Because they've bossed me about, forced me to carry sharp fangs and heavy babies, nagged me to lift my curse and lose my powers, and treated me like I was less important than them because I'm not magical. But soon I'll be alive and they'll be dead, and that's the best magic of all."

"I like the way you think," said Corbie. "I'll let you choose the pecking order. I'll let you watch them die. And afterwards, if you promise to keep your curse forever, I'll let you go free, with both your eyes. Then you can watch us put our mother's plan into action!"

Molly looked along the line of her teammates, lying on the ground, tied up, ready to die. And she wondered if she was making a terrible mistake.

"So, girl, decide who dies first. The tree? The horse? The cat? Or the toad? We'll watch that first death, then you'll choose who's next, and next, and last."

Molly walked along the line, holding the warm bird in her hands. She stopped at Theo and kicked hard at the bottom of his sandals. "It's tempting to choose him. He's bossy, ungrateful, arrogant and far too pleased with himself."

She walked to Innes. "It's tempting to choose him. He's moody, rude, reckless and he tried to drown me last week."

She nudged Atacama. "This sphinx put his job before a promise to me and he sheds hair everywhere."

Then she stood above Beth. "But this self-satisfied

narrow-minded dryad has been nagging me about curses and dark magic ever since we met. She can't forgive me for being descended from a witch and she can't stand watching me enjoy my curse."

Beth was staring up at her. Molly stared back.

Then Molly stepped away to stand beside Corbie, and said loudly, "I'll watch the dryad die first."

Chapter Twenty-six

There was a moment of silence after Molly's announcement, then Beth gasped, "Molly! Please! I didn't—"

"Shut up, Beth," snapped Molly. "It's only a matter of minutes, anyway. You'll die first, then Innes, then Atacama, then Theo. Who goes first isn't that important. Stop whining."

"But…"

Molly glanced along the line again, and wondered if any other tactic could work, apart from picking which of her friends should die first.

She heard Corbie say, "The dryad. Peck the dryad first."

Two curse-hatched women grabbed Beth's wrists and ankles to stretch her out flat on the ground. Molly could see Beth bite her lips tight together as she tried not to scream, and screw her eyelids tight shut as she tried to stop tears escaping. Then Molly saw a dozen crows swoop down to fly in a figure of eight above the dryad. And she saw every beady eye in the circle turn to look at Beth, waiting to watch her struggle and scream and die.

So no one was looking at Theo, as Theo lifted his hands and ripped his ropes apart in a fizzing of flame. No one was looking as he stood up, pulled his plait from his pocket, wrapped it round his upper arm and called out, "STOP!"

Then they *all* looked at him.

Corbie screamed, "Attack him!"

All the crows flew upwards.

Theo yelled, "Molly, get into the centre."

Molly fell forward, cradling the baby bird in her bound hands, as the mass of crows dived at Theo.

Theo lifted both hands and the sky fell in.

The weight of the sky, the huge volume of air, the whole atmosphere, pressed on the birds and forced them to the ground.

Theo pushed his hands down, and the sky darkened from pale blue to bruised purple as the air and light was dragged down to earth. Every curse-hatched – human and feathered – was trapped on the ground, gasping for breath, unable to move.

"Leave these people alone," said Theo calmly. "Leave curse victims alone to lift or break their curses if they can; leave curse-casters alone to regret and reverse their curses if they wish. You poor creatures must live on the power of curses, because you were cursed to do so by your own mother, but you must not extend your curses' natural lives. I will, as I have said, be keeping my eye on you."

He lifted one hand. The human curse-hatched were released. They leapt up and raised their arms to shift and fly. But Theo flicked a finger, and their fringed coats were dragged from their shoulders, then ripped by invisible knives of cold air. The curse-hatched wailed and grabbed at the fabric, but it was shredded into threads and drifted away.

"You will never fly again. You will be earthbound. It's better than you deserve."

Theo lifted the other hand. The sky brightened and the feathered curse-hatched rose from the ground. They all dived towards him, with beaks and claws ready to attack.

Theo laughed and drew an arch in the air.

A rainbow appeared in the sky. It didn't hang motionless above the moor, but folded swiftly downwards. Almost faster than Molly could see, the bright satiny stripes of the rainbow split into ribbons, and the ribbons wove a net. The multi-coloured net wrapped round the cloud of furious crows, then tightened, gathering them together. A bag of birds hung in the air, beaks and wing joints and knobbly feet pushing out between the ribbons.

Theo repeated, "Leave them alone." He flicked a finger and the ribbons rushed through the sky towards the north, black feathers and shocked squawks fluttering from the net as it whirled away.

The dozen curse-hatched who were in human form stood watching, shivering, as their winged army was torn from them.

"I'll drop them in the mouth of the Spey," said Theo. "They'll be waterlogged and unable to fly for a while. But they won't drown."

Corbie ran at him. "I will revenge myself on you!"

Theo pulled the earth out from under Corbie – just the small patches of earth his feet were touching.

Corbie sprawled on the ground, and Theo stood over him.

"No, you won't revenge yourself on me. You can't. I'm too powerful. You must learn your place on the helix of magic. And your place is at the very bottom. If you disturb the balance of the curse arc again, I'll return, and next time I won't make your crows cold and wet. Next time I'll do something much worse. So go back to your dismal wood, wait for your bedraggled army and get used to keeping your head down. And don't you dare bother me or my friends again."

Theo stepped back. The thin crow-girl pulled Corbie to his feet.

Corbie flung himself at Molly instead. "Trickster, liar, mother-murderer!"

Theo sighed. "Right, that's it."

He linked his fingers in a tight curve, and fragments of soil and grit shot up from the ground to form egg shapes, encasing each of the remaining curse-hatched.

Now the curse-hatched were shut inside twelve huge gritty eggs. Theo lifted his right hand and gave the nearest egg a gentle push.

The dozen dirt eggs rolled along the ground in the direction of Stone Egg Wood. Molly could hear muffled yells coming from inside as the eggs rolled faster and faster.

"Earthbound," murmured Theo.

"Trapped forever inside gritty stone eggs," said Innes. "Neat."

"Not forever," said Theo. "The shells will crumble when they reach home. They'll be fine."

"Not completely fine, I hope," said Beth. "They wanted to kill me. Mind you, so did Molly. I thought... I thought we were friends. Why did you choose me?"

Theo crouched by Atacama and sliced through the sphinx's ropes, though Molly couldn't see a knife in his hands.

Molly sat beside Beth. "I'm sorry I scared you. I needed to get their attention away from Theo, to give him a chance to use his plait. I had to choose you, because you were furthest from him."

Beth nodded. "That makes sense. But I still heard you say it. And that will be hard to forget."

Theo said, "Can I cut you loose?"

Molly held her hands up to him. And realised she was still holding the baby bird. It cheeped at her. Her curse-hatched was small and warm and fluffy. And she had kept it safe.

Chapter
Twenty-seven

"Yuck." Beth stared at the small bird. "Another one."

"It's only a baby," said Molly.

Innes said, "So it hasn't pecked out any eyes. Yet. What should we do with it?"

Molly put it gently onto the ground. "I could take it to my aunt's cottage and let her hens bring it up."

But the bird started flapping and waddling after the gritty eggs, towards Stone Egg Wood.

"It's a homing crow," said Innes.

Molly nodded. "That's probably best. I can't hurt it, but it would be hard to love it."

Theo cut the rope round her wrists with a blade of pale flame. Then they were all free, rubbing their wrists and paws, and eyes.

Innes said, "So, that's what a full-strength elemental magician can do with his stored power. Post hundreds of crows in a net to the coast, rip the power of flight from shapeshifters and make it night during the day. All without breaking sweat or turning into a toad. Impressive. How do you do it?"

Theo smiled. "I simply use the power of the world around me. Air, gravity, particles, waves... It's just the manipulation of physics."

"That's how my dad describes shapeshifting." Innes sighed and glanced at the sun. "We'd better go. He'll be turning back very soon, and I only have five minutes to persuade him to make that promise."

His friends followed Innes to a high rock above the river. They sat a few paces away as Innes stood on the rock and looked into the deep pool below.

The water rippled and bubbled, and a glistening grey stallion leapt onto the rock.

The horse flung its front hooves in the air and kicked at Innes, who ducked out of the way. Then the horse changed into a tall man, with jutting eyebrows and long dark-grey hair.

He grabbed Innes by his shoulders and shook him. "You ungrateful treacherous little... Shame on you! How dare you trap me in a rock? Do you know how uncomfortable that is? Do you know how slowly thoughts move through stone? Don't ever do that to me again."

Innes pulled free and stepped back. "It will happen again, very soon. You'll be turned to stone once more in..." he glanced at the sun, "four minutes."

"What?"

"You're still cursed. You'll be free of the stone for five

minutes, every five days. You can't leave the riverside, but you can move and stretch and breathe. And you can lift the curse, during those five minutes, if you promise you will never break the rules, never hunt and kill and eat our neighbours again."

His father shook his head slowly, like it was still as heavy as rock. "Innes? How could you do this? How could you put prey above hunters?"

"I've felt like prey myself a few times this week, and it's not fun. Please make the promise, Dad. It's simple. Promise, then come home."

"Promise to obey rules that deny our essential nature? Never. You're betraying your father, your family and your own future as a hunter. Lift this curse now, or I will never forgive you."

Innes stood firm. "I won't lift it. But you can, by making that promise."

"I will never make that promise. I will never change my mind."

"Neither will I."

Molly watched them, their arms folded, their faces hard and unhappy. She knew there was nothing she or anyone else could do, no one they could outwit or defeat, to solve this problem.

Innes and his father stared at each other in a long cold silence. Then suddenly Innes's father stamped his foot and yelled, "Next time I rise from that water, you'd better be ready, son, because you will be my next prey."

"I might not be here. When you change your mind, you can make your promise to the river, the rocks and the clouds. I've met the Keeper who will hear you, and been in the chamber where your curse will shatter, once you meet the conditions. I don't need to be here. This might be your last chance to look me in the eye and make me that promise."

"Coward. Victim. Prey!"

His dad shifted into a horse, reared up and kicked at Innes's head. But the kick never reached him. Because his father was already a grey granite horse, rearing on the edge of the river.

Innes sighed and shoved the horse with his shoulder. It toppled into the water.

"He's safer in the river," Innes said quietly. "Safer and less obvious." He sat on the rock and stared at the water covering his father.

Everyone else moved over to sit with him.

Beth put her hand on his arm. "Innes, now I've seen how unreasonable your dad is about hunting, I know you didn't have an easy choice. I'm sorry."

Atacama said, "Your father might change his mind next time."

Theo said, "It's a strong curse, for a good reason. You should be proud of it."

Innes didn't reply to any of them.

Molly tried to think of something helpful to say. Then she rose to her feet. Talking wasn't going to cheer Innes up.

"Come on, kelpie. I'll race you."

Molly remembered how she'd shifted in the throne room. She hadn't made or heard a sound. So she knew that this time, she simply had to choose to change into her other self.

She knew that the curse and the hare were now part of her.

"Race you," she repeated. "To that pale rock and back."

Innes looked up. "Will you let me win this time?"

"No. Of course not. If you want to win, you'll have to run faster than me."

She leapt and she ran. A brown blur of fur. And the white horse galloped beside her.

They ran, neck and neck, all the way. They turned at the quartz pillar and raced back together. And they skidded to a halt on the edge of the river.

The hare and the horse stopped at exactly the same moment, in a dead heat.

Molly didn't win.

Innes didn't lose.

Innes grinned.

And past her fur and whiskers, no one could see that Molly was smiling too.

Desperate to find out
what happens next?

Read on for a
sneak preview of

Spellchasers

The Witch's Guide
to Magical Combat

the third and final book
in the trilogy.

Coming
Autumn 2017

Chapter One

When Molly heard her neighbours' cat miaow, she shrank instantly, feeling the familiar flash of heat through her bones.

But when she ran from the noise of the cat, she felt an unfamiliar weight and length whipping around behind her. Did she have a long tail?

She didn't have time to worry about what shape she'd shifted into, because she realised she wasn't running fast enough to get away from a cat. She wasn't leaping and sprinting, she was scuttling and dashing.

Why was she moving so slowly, so weakly?

She glanced round. Yes, she did have a tail. A long, brown, furry tail. At least she wasn't a rat.

But beyond the tail she saw something far more worrying.

The fluffy white cat from next door. Poppet. The cat Molly fed and played with when the Connors were away.

Poppet was stalking her. Belly low, paws stretching forward, eyes fixed on that ridiculous tail.

Molly could run to a gap in the fence, which normally

shifted her back to her girl form, but which might not this time, because the rules of her own personal magic seemed to have shifted today. Or she could hide from the cat now and shift back later, when she wasn't in immediate danger.

Her tiny body decided for her. She desperately wanted to hide. So she darted towards a hole under the shed, which was usually much too small for her. But as a mouse or a vole or a shrew or a whatever she was, she might fit inside.

She ran as fast as she could, on these spindly short legs, with that nonsensical tail and her light body too close to the ground, feeling exposed and vulnerable on the thin winter grass of her back garden.

Suddenly she was aware of the heat and speed of the cat behind her. She felt the air move round her tail as the cat pounced.

Molly veered to her left as the cat's shadow passed over her. The cat's body crashed down onto the patch of grass Molly had been scurrying across a fraction of a second before.

The cat whirled round, trying to work out where her prey had gone, and Molly kept running.

She'd learnt two ways to run in the last four months. Full speed ahead in a straight line, to beat her friend Innes in races. And tricksy leaping and dodging, to evade predators.

So she didn't run straight towards the shed. Even with the smaller body, weaker legs and lesser speed of a tiny rodent, she moved like a hare across the grass: running fast, slowing down, leaping left, dodging right, constantly changing speed and direction.

It wasn't likely that Poppet had ever met a mouse who moved so unpredictably, and Molly kept just out of reach of the cat's claws.

She reached the hole and dived in. She slid right to the back, her tiny heart beating, snug and safe in the cramped dark space.

Molly Drummond was used to suddenly becoming small and fast. But suddenly becoming small and *slow*, that was new and scary.

The noise of a cat had never triggered her curse before. And she'd never become a long-tailed rodent. Normally dog noises triggered the curse; normally she became a hare. But nothing was normal today.

Poppet's paw prodded at the entrance to the hole. Her hot fishy biscuity breath filled the space. The cat was too big to get in, though, and Molly was too far back to be dragged out, so she knew she was safe.

As she crouched, panting and shivering, she wondered what had just happened.

She'd been cursed last autumn by an angry witch, so she turned into a hare (like a bigger stronger faster rabbit) whenever she heard a dog bark or growl. She stayed a hare until she crossed a boundary, usually the boundary between gardens or farms.

She'd learnt how to control the curse, so she could shift into a hare whenever she wanted to, for speed or size or even fun. But she still had to cross a boundary to become a girl again, so she was now an expert on land boundaries in her own Edinburgh neighbourhood, and boundaries in and near the town of Craigvenie, in Speyside, where she'd been cursed.

Molly's curse had been stable and manageable for months, apart from a few days last year when the witch had altered her curse so it was harder to shift back. Until today.

So she'd better go north, to see if the Craigvenie friends whose curses she'd lifted last year could help her, and to work out why her curse had become more dangerous. But she couldn't go to Speyside until she got out from under this shed and became a girl again.

Molly shivered as she watched Poppet's paw withdraw at last. If the rules or strength of her curse had somehow changed, perhaps crossing a boundary wouldn't shift her back?

She crouched in the dark, wondering what it would be like to be this trembling and terrified creature forever. Trying to cross a boundary was the only way to find out. Even if there was still a cat out there.

She moved to the entrance of the hole, her whiskers snuffling and jerking. She couldn't smell cat breath. She couldn't sense animal heat or hear a huge heartbeat.

Poppet had probably given up. It was probably safe.

Molly hesitated. She didn't want to leave the security of this dusty dark hole. She gathered up all the courage she could find in her tiny shaking body, dashed out and ran for the gap in the fence.

A white shape leapt from the shed roof, bounded onto the top of the fence and landed on the grass, paw slashing down to trap the tiny form on the ground.

And Poppet scratched the knuckle of Molly's human thumb.

The cat backed off, white fur standing up along her spine.

Molly smiled. "Sorry to give you a fright, Poppet."

She climbed over the wooden fence and ran to her back door, hoping the cat wouldn't miaow before she got inside.

She rushed into the living room. "Mum! Dad! Can I go to Aunt Doreen's next week, for the February holidays?"

Her mum said, "Again? You stayed with Doreen last tattie holidays and complained the whole way up the A9. But then you pestered us to take you up at Christmas, and now you want to go again next week? What's in Speyside that you can't get in Edinburgh?"

"My friends in Craigvenie," said Molly. But she was also thinking about the magic she'd found up north. She needed a chance to break this curse or it might kill her before she got to secondary school.

She looked at her dad. "We play in the woods, by the rivers and in the hills, like you did when you were wee."

He smiled. "It's a good place to grow up. If the snow holds off, I'll drive you there."

So Molly went upstairs to pack, and to work out how to avoid cats as well as dogs for the next three days.

Chapter Two

Molly said hi to her Aunt Doreen and bye to her dad, who was having a scone before driving home, then she threw her bag into the tiny sloped-ceiling bedroom and went back outside to fetch her bike from the boot of the car.

She cycled through Craigvenie and ran through the wood to her best friend Beth's house. Beth's Aunt Jean said, "She's gone up into the hills with Innes and Atacama. They've just left, you might catch them."

Molly cycled fast on the road leading towards the snow-topped mountains in the distance, then more slowly over the moorland paths.

If Innes had galloped enthusiastically the whole way, she'd never have caught up. But eventually she saw her friends ahead of her.

Beth, the dryad, with her silver jewellery glinting in the cold sunlight, purple hair and black clothes. Innes, the kelpie, in his blond-haired, jeans-wearing boy form, rather than his white-maned horse form. And

Atacama, the sphinx, looking like a puma-sized black cat, apart from the small wings on his back and his long almost-human face.

"Hey!" Molly yelled. "Wait for me!"

When she reached them, she jumped off her bike and laid it in the heather.

Beth hugged her. "We didn't think you were coming back until Easter."

"I need your help, because my curse has gone weird. Come over to this burn and I'll show you. It's a boundary, isn't it?"

They all nodded.

Molly stood on the edge of the narrow burn. "Atacama, make a cat noise."

"Don't be so insulting."

"Just as an experiment. Please."

He purred, lighter and softer than his normal big cat rattle.

Molly became a mouse, jumped into the shockingly cold water, paddled across and pulled herself out on the other side, as a girl.

She turned round. Beth looked worried, Innes was frowning and Atacama had his usual stony calm face.

Molly said, "Now, Beth, hoot like an owl."

Beth made a long eerie noise like the owls that swooped through her birch trees at night.

Molly shifted into another tiny rodent, with less tail. She wondered if she was a vole as she swam back across the burn.

"It's not just rodents," she said, after she'd shifted to a

girl again. "Can you do a smaller bird, Beth, a thrush or something?"

Beth sang a quick trill of notes.

And Molly became something she'd never been before. Something legless and spineless. She felt fingers pick her up and carry her over the boundary, then she fell to the ground.

"A worm?" snapped Beth. "Really? You wanted me to turn you into a worm?"

Molly shook her head. "I expected to become a snail: that's what happened when I heard birdsong in the garden on Thursday. Anyway, this is how my curse has gone weird. Whatever predator I hear, I become its prey. Mousey things, creepy crawlies, all sorts of little edible creatures. It's risky being too far from a boundary, because I can't sprint as most of these animals. Though sometimes it might be fun. Can anyone do a convincing wolf?"

Innes raised his face to the sky and howled.

Molly became a slim long-legged deer.

Before she crossed the water, she turned away from her friends and bounded across the heather just to enjoy the speed, the smells, the drumming of hooves on the ground. Then she leapt the burn, rolled over and jumped up as a girl.

Innes laughed.

Molly grinned. "It's only the hare I can choose to become. It seems all the other animals have to be triggered by a noise outside me. But I haven't experimented. It's too dangerous on my own."

"Molly, that's horrible," said Beth.

Innes said, "It's not horrible. It's amazing! You can shapeshift into lots more animals than I can. Most of which I'm going to thrash in a race. A horse against a mouse or a worm, that's going to be so easy. I'm going to win everything this holiday!"

"No more races!" said Beth. "You can't stay like this, Molly. You have to get rid of this curse. You surely don't want to be a worm ever again?"

"I didn't want to be a worm that time."

Beth frowned. "This wouldn't have happened if you'd truly committed to doing whatever is necessary to lift your curse."

"Whatever is necessary? Like becoming a witch? You know the only way I can force Mr Crottel to lift the curse is to beat him in magical combat, and the only way I can do that is to embrace my family's ancient heritage and become a witch. But given the choice between being a part-time hare or a full-time witch, I think the cursed hare is a better option."

"And that's handy for you, because you like being a hare," said Beth.

"Yes, I do. It's inconvenient and dangerous, but if I hadn't been cursed I wouldn't have met all of you. Also, I get to beat Innes in races."

"You don't always beat me, sometimes we cross the finish line together."

"That's only happened once. You've never actually won. So, I'm good at being a hare and I enjoy it, most of the time. But I feel really vulnerable as a tiny rodent, and when I'm not a mammal I feel like I might forget about my real self and forget to cross a boundary. Which means I think Beth is probably right now: I need to find a way to get rid of the curse."

Innes said, "When you helped us lift our curses, we promised to help you lift yours. So if you're sure this is what you want...?"

Molly nodded at him.

"...then I will help you break your curse."

"Me too," said Beth.

"And me," said Atacama.

TO BE CONTINUED...

Will Molly finally break her curse?

The Witch's Guide to Magical Combat

COMING AUTUMN 2017

Discover the story
behind Molly's curse

BY THE AWARD-WINNING AUTHOR OF
THE FABLED BEAST CHRONICLES

Spellchasers

The Beginner's Guide
to Curses

LARI
DON

Molly hesitated. "Are you cursed?"
The girl nodded. "Aren't you?"

Curses aren't real. Magic is only in stories. So Molly Drummond definitely can't be magically cursed. Can she?

When Molly finds herself in a curse-lifting workshop with four magical classmates – a kelpie, a dryad, a sphinx and a toad – she's determined not to believe in it.

But it's true that whenever a dog barks, Molly suddenly becomes a small and very fast hare... How long can she keep not believing?

Follow Molly into a world of brilliant magic, unexpected adventure and extraordinary friendship in the first book of Lari Don's breathtaking *Spellchasers* trilogy.

"Exciting, thrilling and breathtaking." Emily, age 9

"What more could you want from a book?" Tomasz, age 11

"Absolutely brilliant." Isabel, age 9

Also by Lari Don

FABLED BEAST CHRONICLES

It's not every day a grumpy, injured centaur appears on your doorstep. And that's just the beginning...

Helen's first aid kit comes in very handy when she meets Yann's friends – a fairy, a dragon, a phoenix, a werewolf and even a selkie – who have a habit of getting into trouble.

Together they must solve riddles, fight fauns and defeat the dangerous Master of the Maze before midwinter and the end of the world.

"A gripping fairytale that will keep you reading past your bedtime" Cait, age 8

Including
First Aid for Fairies and Other Fabled Beasts
WINNER OF A SCOTTISH CHILDREN'S BOOK AWARD

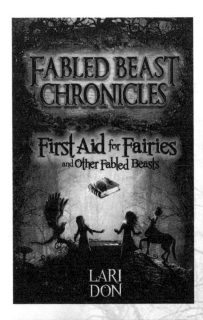

FABLED BEAST
CHRONICLES

First Aid for Fairies
and Other Fabled Beasts

LARI
DON

FABLED BEAST
CHRONICLES

Wolf Notes
and
Other Musical Mishaps

LARI
DON

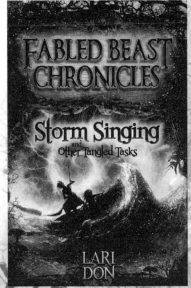

FABLED BEAST
CHRONICLES

Storm Singing
and
Other Tangled Tasks

LARI
DON

FABLED BEAST
CHRONICLES

Maze Running
and
Other Magical Missions

LARI
DON

EMBRACE THE MAGIC.
DEFY DESTINY.

One sunny morning the triplets disappear,
leaving only a few mysterious clues behind.

Older sister Pearl sets out to find them. Her journey
unfolds into an incredible and perilous adventure.

Can Pearl save her brother and sisters
from the unknown fate that lies ahead?